Lot Lizards

FRED GREENE

LOT LIZARDS

iUniverse books may be ordered through booksellers or by contacting:

iUniverse
1663 Liberty Drive
Bloomington, IN 47403
www.iuniverse.com
844-349-9409

Because of the dynamic nature of the Internet, any web addresses or links contained in this book may have changed since publication and may no longer be valid. The views expressed in this work are solely those of the author and do not necessarily reflect the views of the publisher, and the publisher hereby disclaims any responsibility for them.

Any people depicted in stock imagery provided by Getty Images are models, and such images are being used for illustrative purposes only.
Certain stock imagery © Getty Images.

Author Credits : Heath Dobson

ISBN: 978-1-6632-3233-5 (sc)
ISBN: 978-1-6632-3234-2 (hc)
ISBN: 978-1-6632-3235-9 (e)

Library of Congress Control Number: 2021923721

Print information available on the last page.

iUniverse rev. date: 11/29/2021

Disclaimer

If any of the characters or story depicted in this novel appear to be similar to real life persons, places, or things, it is pure coincidental. The novel is completely fictional written by the author who drove a big rig over the road for a number of years. The storyline is from his experiences and from stories he heard from other truck drivers. The novel was written about truck drivers for truck drivers and that is the reason for the profanity and all the fighting and sex in the book. It is what truck drivers like to talk about and read about.

Chapter One

Buck Johnson was walking from the motor pool at Camp LeJeune to the re-enlistment office. It was part of the out processing when a marine left the Corps. Buck had been a "jarhead" for the past three years and he was ready to get out of the Marine Corps. He had not had real bad duty and he toyed with the idea of staying in for another term. In his analysis there were two main reasons for not staying in for another term. If he stayed in, he would likely have another deployment to Afghanistan or somewhere in the Middle East. He had served one tour in Afghanistan and he did not relish the idea of serving another one. The other reason was during his time in the service he had become a pretty good boxer. After he returned from his tour in Afghanistan, when he was not driving trucks and tractor trailers, the majority of his time was spent in the gym training for boxing matches. The marine Corps had done two good things for Buck. They had made him into a good truck driver and a good boxer.

Buck had a record of 12-1, 3 by knock out. His one loss was to the post champion of Camp Lejeune, a guy named "Killer McGee," who went on to be a professional boxer. That fight was enough to convince Buck he did not want to fight professionally. He had some promoters interested in training him and booking him in professional bouts. After the fight with "Killer McGee" he had had enough boxing. Buck had not really wanted to fight him in the first place. "Killer McGee" had a reputation of not just wanting to beat his opponent, but to kill or maim him for life. He was also a heavy weight and Buck was a middle weight boxer. Buck let his buddies put him up to it, because they thought he could be the post champion and there were a lot of perks to being the post champion. Normal military duty ceased for the post champion. All he had to do was go to the gym every day and train. He had to be ready to represent the post against another post at any time and along with that went a lot of freedom from normal military duty.

Buck had got into a fight at the motor pool one day with an older black guy named Mack. First Sgt. Timms, who was over the motor pool told Buck to take a tanker over to the fuel storage facility and fill it up. Buck jumped into the tanker and did what he was told. When he got back, Mack asked him, "Hey Dickhead, why the hell did you run off with my field jacket in my truck? Did you not see it lying on the seat? I have been driving that truck and I was going to fill it up myself when I got back from taking a shit. I have to take it out to the ranger station to give them some fuel."

Mack's attitude did not sit well with Buck. Buck fired back, "I was just doing what "Top" told me to do. I did not see any name on the truck. If you want to make something of it, my ass is just like a salad patch. You can get a mess any time you want to."

Mack says "Fuck you. You little smart ass. I'll mop this floor up with you."

By this time, they were hollering at each other and Sgt. Timms jumped in, "If you guys are going to fight, lets do this right. We will go down to the gym and put the gloves on and you guys can fight until the cows come home. We got work to do now. Be down at the gym at 1700 hours. I'll get it set up for you. Right now, get your asses to work."

"I'll be there," said Mack. "Me too," said Buck.

When Buck got to the gym at 1700 hours, the boxing ring was all set up. Boxing gloves were hanging on a rack and the gym manager told him to get some gloves and put on some trunks if he did not have any.

Mack was already in the ring ready to go. The word had gotten around and there were probably 30 spectators in the bleachers to watch this event. Buck went back into the locker room and got ready. He had thought about this all day. Mack was a big black guy about 35. A lifer (career soldier). He was about 240 pounds and had a pot gut He was muscular but moved very slow. Buck was about 200 pounds and very fit. The Marine Core had seen to that. He was not afraid of Mack. He planned to dance around Mack and sucker punch him when he saw an opening. He planned to work on his fat gut whenever he could.

When Buck climbed into the ring, he saw his buddy, Billy, from the motor pool in the corner holding a water bottle and a towel. Billy said, "Buck, you can beat this guy. Get in there and whip his ass. I never liked him, anyway."

The referee brought the two boxers to the middle of the ring. He said they would run the match just like a regular boxing match with three minute rounds. He said, "Keep it clean and may the best man win."

Buck's plan worked to perfection. When the bell rung, Mack charged at Buck like a wild bull. Buck danced around him and hit him hard in the side of the head. He kept coming at Buck and Buck kept dancing around and punching him in the stomach and in the head. At one point Mack tried to grab Buck and tackle him. The referee broke that up and separated them. "This is a boxing match," he said, "not a wrestling match."

The fight did not go past three rounds. Mack had never fought a real boxing match. Boxing seemed to come naturally to Buck. He had worked out on a punching bag at the gym and he was in such good shape compared to Mack. At the end of every round, Billy was in his corner giving him water and wiping the sweat off with a towel. He kept saying "Keep up what you are doing. He is wearing down. Everybody in here is pulling for you." When the bell rang for the third round, Buck landed a solid punch to the side of Mack's temple. This visibly stunned Mack. Then Buck went hard to Mack's gut with a series of blows. Mack was bent over from all the blows to his stomach and when Buck came up with an uppercut to Mack's chin, Mack went down. The referee came over to do a count. But Mack held up his hand and said, "That is enough for me. I am done." He stumbled to his feet and said, "You are good Buck, you should be a boxer. I am no match for you. I am a street fighter. There is a big difference. You should try to get some boxing matches. The Marines are always looking for good boxers. You could be great, I think. I hope there are no hard feelings between you and me. We have to work together at the motor pool."

"I am good. No hard feelings," replied Buck.

After that fight with Mack, the gym manager, a guy named Ralph talked with Buck. He said, "I can get you hooked up with Sam. He is the boxing trainer on the post. He will work with you and get you set up with some matches with other boxers at your level. I think you could be very good with some training and a work out program for boxing. It will get you out of your regular duty. You can spend a lot more time in the gym than down at the motor pool. What do you say?"

Buck replied, "Sounds good to me. I like to work out. I have been having to do it on my own time. If this can get me out of my work at the motor pool, I'm in. Thanks."

Ralph told Buck, "I'll talk with Sam and see what he says. I am sure he will be interested. He is always looking for new boxing talent. He has trained some good boxers in the past. Several of his boxers have gone on and fought professionally. His best boxer on the post now is a guy named "Killer McGee." I am sure if McGee gets out of the service, he can fight professionally if he wants to. I'll get back with you."

"Okay," says Buck.

A few days later Buck word came down to the motor pool for Buck to meet Sam at the gym at 1700 hours that afternoon. Buck met with Sam and Sam explained, "I would like to work with you. I can make a boxer out of you. I have already talked with Sgt. Timms at the motor pool and all the guys there are behind you. They all want to see you fight some more; it seems like. Even Mack. He seems like he is your biggest fan now. What do you think? Are you interested?"

"Yeah, I have two more years in the Marines. I'll give it a shot."

"I need you to report the main gym near the NCO club tomorrow at 0800 and we will start work.""

Buck nodded, "I'll be there."

Buck got to the gym the next day about 15 minutes before 0800. He could tell right away that this gym was for boxers. There were about twelve or so boxers already working out. Some were punching bags. Some were jumping rope. Some were lifting weights. There were three rings and a couple of boxers were sparring in one of them. Buck watched them for a while and thought he could beat either one of them. Sam saw Buck and came over to greet him. Sam showed him around the gym and introduced him to some of the boxers that were training. He gave Buck a locker that already had trousers, boxing shoes, and gloves. He told him to get dressed for his workout and meet him at the speed bag. Sam had Buck work out on the bag and jump rope. Buck also lifted some weights. Buck was already convinced he would rather do this than work at the motor pool.

Buck trained hard and progressed really fast. Sam got Buck some matches with boxers at Camp LeJeune and some bouts with boxers from other posts. Buck won his first twelve matches and Sam said he would schedule a match with "Killer McGee." Buck did not think he was ready for "Killer McGee." Buck had watched him in the gym sparring with other boxers but the two of them had never got in the ring together. Buck had a more than healthy respect for "Killer McGee." He had downright fear of him. All the guys from the motor pool had been coming to all of Buck's boxing matches and were real supporters of him. His buddy, Billy, was in his corner for every fight encouraging him. Billy told him, "You are ready for "Killer." You just need to be smart. "Killer McGee" is bigger and has a real knockout punch. You need to stay away from him the first few rounds and let him get tired. You are in much better shape than he is and he does not have the power in his punches after he gets tired. You will have to rely on quickness and stamina to win the match and you need to plan on going twelve rounds with him."

"Okay, said Buck, Sam said he would schedule the fight in five weeks to let the boxers get ready and advertise it for a few weeks so there would be a good crowd. I'll go to work. I need to get better at bobbing and weaving and my foot work needs to be quicker. I know how to work on those things."

Buck worked hard for the next few weeks and he tried to avoid watching "Killer." Buck could tell "Killer" was getting ready for him. "Killer" had much more intensity in his workouts. About two weeks before the match, "Killer" confronted Buck. "Do you think a little punk kid like you can beat me? I have fought plenty of guys like you. They all thought they could take me down. I'll knock you out in the first round and mop the floor up with you."

Buck did not know where it came from or why, but he simply said "Go for it."

From that point on, Buck developed the confidence he needed to get in the ring with "Killer." Buck got Sam and Billy to work with him and he scheduled his time in the gym when "Killer" was not there. He did a lot of running to build up his stamina. Sam and Billy encouraged him all the way and said he was ready. They both said he could beat "Killer" if he fought smart and had confidence he could go the distance with him. Very few fighters had gone the distance with "Killer." His record was mostly knockouts in the early rounds.

The gym was packed the night of the fight. "Killer McGee" had been the post champion for two years and had never been beaten. The crowd was looking for a good fight and the majority of the crowd was pulling for Buck. Billy was in Buck's corner as usual. Sam had to appear neutral since he was in charge of the fight and he represented both boxers, but Buck knew he was really in his corner too.

Sam was the ring announcer and he went to the center of the ring, "Welcome to the Camp LeJeune boxing arena and to this fight tonight for the Post championship. The current Post Champion is "Killer McGee" weighing in at 245 pounds and his opponent is Buck Johnson weighing in at 225 pounds. The referee in charge of the fight is Johnny Cox. So, you boxers come to the center of the ring and LET'S GET READY TO RUMBLE."

The boxers came to the center of the ring and met with the referee. Buck and "Killer" were staring each other down and Buck really had no idea what the referee was saying, because he was so focused on what he had to do. The referee said, "Let's have a clean fight. No low punches, no head knocking, no dirty fighting and stop when the bell rings. Now, touch gloves and come out boxing."

The bell rang and "Killer" came charging out just as Buck thought he would. He came straight at Buck and tried to land a big haymaker right away. Buck danced around the ring and made "Killer" miss with all his power punches. They traded blows for the entire round. Neither boxer did a lot of damage to the other boxer. Most of the blows were blocked by the gloves as both boxers held their gloves high protecting their face. Buck got a few body shots into the side of "Killer" as he danced around him. "Killer" got one counter punch in on Buck and Buck felt it. He had never been hit that hard. He was surprised by the power of the blow. He had to back away and keep his distance from "Killer" until the stars in his eyes went away. The bell rang and Buck was glad he survived the first round.

He went to the corner and Billy encouraged him, "That was a good round, Buck. I saw that one blow he landed dazed you, but you danced around after that to avoid any knock out punches. Just keep it up in two more rounds. He will begin to wear down. Stay away from him and keep dodging his punches for two more rounds at least. I know you are not as tired as he is."

"He hits hard. I have never been hit as hard as he hits," Buck replied.

The bell rang for the second round and "Killer" came out swinging. He was still trying to land the big KO punch and end this fight. Buck kept dancing around "Killer" and preventing from landed a real solid blow. They were exchanging punches and Buck knew he was in a fight. Buck also knew he was probably not winning theses first two rounds on points either. He needed to land more scoring punches. Buck made it through the second round. The first six rounds were much the same. The boxers traded punches and both boxers were getting beat up pretty bad Buck had a slight cut over his left eye and his eyes were swollen. 'Killer" did not have any cuts, but his face was getting swollen. At one point "Killer" seemed to be so frustrated, he tried to grab Buck and throw him down. The referee stopped him and warned him this was a boxing match and not a wrestling match. In the seventh round, Buck tried to throw a punch to "Killer's" head and got caught with a hard counter punch that stunned him. "Killer" then threw another roundhouse that knocked Buck to the mat. Buck was dazed and realized that the referee was counting him out. Buck grabbed the ropes and stumbled to his feet by the count of seven. The referee looked into Buck's eyes and asked him if he wanted to continue the fight. Buck said "Hell Yes!" He was mad now. Mad at himself and mad at "Killer."

The bell rang before "Killer" could inflict anymore damage. Buck went to his corner and Billy said, "Listen, Buck, you have shown you can go toe to toe with this guy. You do not have to continue to get beat up. We can throw in the towel right now if you want to. I almost did it when you got knocked down, but I knew the round was almost over."

"Don't you dare end this fight. I might not win it, but I am going to go the distance with this guy and he is going to know he was in a fight. I am through dancing around this guy. I am going after him now WIN OR LOSE."

The bell rang for round number eight and Buck looked like a different fighter. Buck went after "Killer." He was throwing punches left and right. "Killer" seemed tired and defenseless at times. They both were landing punches and it was a good boxing match. If you were scoring the rounds fairly, I am sure Buck won rounds eight, nine, ten and eleven. After the eleventh round, Buck went to the corner and Billy said, "Buck, I think this match is really close. You need to win this round convincingly. It is the last round. Go out there and get him. You can do it."

The bell rang for the twelfth and final round and the two fighters went to the center of the ring and started punching. They were both tired, but it was apparent that "Killer" was more tired than Buck. They were toe to toe and trading punches. Buck then pulled away and circled "Killer" and caught him with a right to the forehead and "Killer" stumbled. Buck went after him when he saw he had hurt "Killer." Buck threw a couple of more punches to the head and "Killer" spun around and went down. The referee ruled it a slip, but everybody in the gym knew it was a knockdown. Buck got madder and when "Killer" got up he went straight for him and threw punches like he had never thrown before. Some of them landed but most of them were blocked by gloves or were body shots.

The final bell rang and the referee stopped the fight. The faces of both boxers looked like they had been run through a meatgrinder. Sam called the boxers to the center of the ring to announce the score of the fight. Then he said, "We have to score cards to determine the results of the match. We have a split decision. Judge Pearson scored the fight 105 – 100 for "Killer McGee." Judge Frederick scored the fight 110 – 100 for Buck Johnson, and referee Cox scored the fight 108 – 100 for

"Killer McGee," the winner and still Post Champion. Sam raised the arm of "Killer McGee" to a chorus of boos from the audience of fight fans. The referee was obviously biased in favor of "Killer McGee." He had already ruled an obvious knockdown as a slip.

Buck accepted the decision and chalked it up to Post politics. He felt he had won the fight. The fight made him realize he did not want to box anymore. He had had enough. He had seen enough cauliflower ears and scarred up faces to convince him that it was not a life that he wanted. Buck was a good-looking young man and he did not want to take a chance on damaging his good looks even though a lot of the fight promoters thought with the proper training and management, he could really make a real good living at professional boxing.

And that is exactly what Buck was thinking as he went into the re-enlistment office. The re-enlistment officer wanted to sign Buck up for another three years. He went on further to say, "If you will re-enlist, all you will be doing is boxing and training to box. I saw your fight with "Killer McGee" and I did not think there was any doubt that you won the fight. I guess it is difficult to overcome the current Post Champion and his reputation. I thought you fought a helluva fight."

Buck replied, "He was tough. I had never been hit like he hit me. I was undefeated in twelve fights before that one and it convinced me that fight for a living was not something I want to do. I had to not do anything for four weeks to let my wounds heal from that fight."

"What do you want to do when you get out of the Marines?"

Buck said, "I want to drive a big rig. The Marines have taught me how to drive a truck and that is what I plan to do."

"Well, Okay, if I cannot talk you into staying in the corps, then I wish you the best of luck in truck driving or whatever you decide to do."

Chapter Two

Buck Johnson was in his second week of his on the job training on a big rig. He was team driving with his mentor, Big John Patrick. John was an owner operator of a big rig which was leased to Whiteline Freight. Whiteline freight was a nationwide truckload company with over 20,000 trucks hauling freight in all 48 states. They were delivering a load of tires to a Michelin plant in Reno, Nevada. When the truck was unloaded, Big John sent Buck back to get the signed bill of laden from the consignee. Buck was still learning about trucking, but he had already learned that a signed bill of laden was necessary to confirm delivery of the load and to authorize payment for the delivery, and never to leave a site after being unloaded without one. Buck got his signed bill of laden and asked the gentleman who signed the bill where they could get something good to eat. It was about 1700 hours (EST) and they had been driving all day and they were pretty hungry. The snacks on the truck were not nearly as appealing as a fresh cooked meal.

The ruddy faced gentleman at the loading dock said, "There is a diner right up the road that has a good meat and three plate for supper." Then he added, "Just past the diner is the cathouse. Most of the truckers like to know about that." He said, "If you look up to the top of the hill, you can see the red light from here." Buck rushed back to the cab of the eighteen wheeler with this wealth of information he had gathered.

"John," Buck said with enthusiasm, "the man at the dock said there was a diner just up the road that had a good plate dinner. He also told me that there was a cathouse just past the diner. Can we go?" John contemplated for a moment. Then he says, "Well, maybe you deserve a reward for your good driving. We'll certainly get something to eat and I will take you up to the whorehouse. I don't plan on spending any of my money on hookers, but I'll take you up there and wait on you if you have the money and you want to spend it."

Big John was 45 years old and had a wife and two kids at home in North Carolina and he had had his share of road whores, and was not as eager as Buck was to visit the whorehouse. Buck was 23 years old and had never been to a whorehouse. Buck was getting more excited by the minute in anticipation of things to come. Big John had taken into consideration that they had left South Carolina only two days earlier and had delivered the load ahead of schedule. He would have to set their PTA (projected time of availability) out a few hours, but that would not be a problem since it was a Saturday night and chances were that they might not get sent a load assignment to the on board computer (referred to as the Qualcomm) until the next day. John also took into consideration that this "young buck" he was traveling with would not be in the cathouse very long.

There was plenty of truck parking at the diner which is always a big consideration when one is driving a big rig. Truckers don't always go where the best food is; sometimes they go where they can park their rig and the quality of the food actually being less important than the good parking space. But in this case, the diner offered both good parking and good food. There were about eight trucks lined up in a row beside the diner and plenty of room for one more. Big John pulled in beside an owner operator Kenworth rig pulling a reefer. If they had been spending the night there, he might not have parked beside the reefer because they can make a lot of noise and keep drivers awake as the refrigeration turns unit on and off.

John and Buck went inside the diner and sat at a vacant table. Buck ordered the meatloaf and John got the country style steak. John and

Buck agreed the food tasted good. A cowboy trucker was sitting at the next table. Buck noticed that he was wearing a cowboy hat and boots and jeans with a big belt buckle. Buck thought he was dressed for bull riding instead of trucking. Buck figured that he could tell that Big John was training Buck because of the trainer shirt that John was wearing. He asked Buck, "Are you learning to drive a truck? " The cocky Buck answered, "I have been driving trucks and tractors all my life. Why, I am teaching this old man a thing or two. "The cowboy trucker asked Big John if that was right. John replied, "This little whipper snapper is still wet behind the ears and he has a lot to learn. He better not be so cocky. He does not know me. I'll drop him off at the next bus station and send him home if his attitude does not change. "The cowboy trucker went on to say, "I kinda thought that was the way it was. By the way if you guys are going east on Interstate 80, there is a bad wreck on the eastbound side at mile marker 150 before you get to Winnemucca. Traffic was backed up for about 6-7 miles. I think a big truck got tangled up with a travel trailer and had both lanes blocked. I am glad I was traveling west on Interstate 80. It would have sure made me late for my load." Big John says, "It will probably be cleared up by the time we get on the road. I told my trainee I would take him up to the cathouse and let him spend his money on the pros if he wanted to." The cowboy trucker replied, "You watch out boy, don't take any more money in there than you need. It will cost you about $300-400. Those women got ways to get all your money if you are not careful. I hear there are some good looking women in there, the driver said with a wink. You be sure to wear a rubber. You don't want to catch anything you can't get rid of."

Big John added, "Don't you stay in there very long. We don't have a load yet, but we could get one anytime. Let's go if you think you are ready." Buck was more than ready. He could not wait to see what the hookers looked like and to get his horns trimmed (he was very horny since the last time he had gotten laid was back home in South Carolina about two weeks ago). Big John drove the big truck up to the cathouse and parked beside it. There was a big lot with a lot of room to park his rig. John says, "I am crawling into the sleeper to catch some shut eye. Go have a big time and hurry back."

Buck went up to the door of the cathouse with much anticipation and some fear of the unknown. He opened the door and walked into a big room with several scantily clad women in it. There was an adjoining room with what looked like a bar and a pool table in it. An older lady came up to Buck and said, "Hello young man, what are you interested in tonight? Are you interested in some female companionship? We have a lot of very fine looking ladies here to serve you tonight. Would you like to have a look at all of them?"

Buck tried to act like he was in complete control and says, "Sure, let's have a look at them."

He then heard a bell ring and shortly thereafter 12 or so women came into the room and lined up in a row. There was a big variety black, white, Latin and oriental flavors. The first lady in the line-up had a black leather outfit on and tattoos all over her and she was holding a cat of nine tails in her hand and slapping it into her other hand. Buck considered what she might be like and decided she might be into a little too much sadism and masochism. He looked down the line and was really having a hard time making up his mind. The Madame encouraged him to pick one, "Pick one out young man, these ladies want to go back to sleep. You woke them up to come in here and see you. I am going to tell them all to go back to bed if you do not hurry up and make up your mind." She paused for a brief period and when Buck still did not pick one, she "Okay ladies, you can go, I do not think he is interested."

Buck then panicked and said, "How about the one in the red baby doll outfit toward the end of the line?" Buck had checked her out pretty close and she had a kind of "girl next door" look and Buck really was not into anything kinky. He just wanted some straight sex - a little sucking and fucking. The girl in the red baby doll pajamas came back to Buck.

The closer she came, the better she looked to Buck. And when she got real close, he could smell how good she smelled. "Did you pick me? I was not sure you meant me."

"Yes I meant you." Buck tried to act nonchalant as he answered her.

The girl said, "My name is Candy. Let's go back to my room and talk about what I can do for you." She took Buck by the hand a led him down a hallway to a small dimly lit bedroom. When she got to the room they sat down on the bed and Brandy said,"

What are you interested in tonight?"

Buck tried to act experienced in these matters and replied, "I would just like some normal sex - some good old sucking and fucking. I am not sure if I can afford it though?"

Candy pointed to her mouth "for this" and then to her pussy and said, "and for this, it will be $200 for the house and $300 for me."

Buck reached in his pocket for his billfold and pulled out five 100 dollar bills. He kept these in the hidden compartment in his billfold for just these sorts of *emergency* situations. Brandy took the money and said, "I have to pay the house before we can get started."

Buck asked her, "Do you mind if I take a shower, so I will be fresh and clean for you?

We have been driving for two three days and I probably need one."

"Sure you can. There are towels hanging beside the shower stall and soap in the shower. Help yourself. Go ahead and get comfortable and I will be right back," said Candy as she headed out of the room.

Buck cleaned himself real good in the shower and was sitting on the edge of the bed with nothing on but the towel he wrapped around his waist when Candy returned. Candy sat down on the bed beside Buck. She could tell he was already excited by the way the towel was sticking up under the pressure of a fully erect cock. She stuck her hand inside the towel gave Buck's member a squeeze. Brandy was pleasantly surprised by the size of Buck's cock. Buck was larger than the average at a solid eight and a half inches. Candy said, "OOOh, you are big. I don't know if I can handle this big thing." She proceeded to remove the towel from around Buck and placed it on the table beside the bed. She then leaned down to Bucks cock and gave it a real good visual inspection and then she put her nose down to the tip of the cock and smelled it. Buck did not mind at all that she was cautious. It made him feel more at ease. Buck watched her take out a rubber and open it up. She placed it on the head of his dick and as she rolled it down the shaft, she moved her mouth down the length of the shaft at the same time. She could not quite get the entire length of the cock into her warm mouth.

Buck could not help himself. He lay back on the bed and said, "Gawd, that feels good. You really know how to make my dick feel good." She continued to give Buck head until she thought he was good and ready to fuck. Brandy said, "Are you ready to fuck?" How do you want me?" Buck had thought about this ahead of time and said, "I want you to sit on my dick first and then we can do it doggie style and then I will get on top of you and finish. Is that okay with you?"

Candy replied, "We can try it. I may not be able to take that big thing on top, but I will try. Let me get up on top of you. Candy took off her baby doll pajamas and got up on top of Buck and inserted his dick into her pussy. She started out real slow and then she got a little faster. She was not able to go all the way down on the long dick, but it still felt good to Buck. "You just lie there, she said, "and let me do the work."

She really had a tight pussy and Buck could tell he was not going to last very long before he climaxed. He kept saying 'Gawd, that feels so good." After just a few minutes in this position, Buck said, "Turn over, I want to get behind you"

Candy rolled off him and got on her hands and knees on top of the bed. Buck maneuvered around behind Candy and pushed his dick into her tight pussy from the rear. From this position, Buck could look down at Candy's firm butt. Buck said, "You have a beautiful butt. You must work out. Gawd, you feel good. You are going to make me cum."

"Go ahead, I want it. I want to feel you cum."

Buck was trying to make it last, but he knew he was not going to be able to last. He started trying to think about something else. He tried thinking about driving a truck, working out math problems, anything to make this feeling last a little longer. It felt too good. He could feel the pressure building deep in his groin area. He wanted to stop and turn her over but he could not stop the mounting crescendo of excitement. Before he realized what was happening, He was squirting cum into the rubber. He made a final lunge deep into Candy's pussy and held it there until he was finished cumming. It must have been 8-10 blasts of cum he felt and he knew he had filled up the tip off the rubber and more.

He pulled his dick out and they both inspected the rubber to make sure it had not burst. "Boy you got a lot of cum out of me." Buck said as they both saw a good 4-5 tablespoons of cum in the tip of the rubber. Buck laid down flat on his back and Brandy proceeded to gently pull the cum filled rubber off and throw it in the waste basket beside the bed. She then took a warm rag and wiped the excess cum off his dick and surrounding area.

Buck could not help but say, "Gawd, you sure took care of me. I have never been so satisfied in my life. You completely drained the sperm back up I had."

Candy said, "I am glad. I always like a satisfied customer. I hope you will come back and see me. I am only doing this to save up enough money to pay my way through nursing school and I won't be doing it anymore after that."

"You can count on that." Buck replied. Buck's endorphins were raging. He was sort of infatuated with Candy for an instant. He thought occurred to him that Candy might be someone to take home to meet his mother. Then he quickly came back to his senses. He knew that could never happen. He really did hope he could come back sometime. He still had at least one more position that he did not get to try out on Brandy.

Buck was feeling real good as he put his clothes back on and headed out to the truck. When he got back to the truck, John crawled out of the sleeper and said, "Let's go boy, we got a load we have got to pick up in Carson City. I really did not think you would have taken as long as you did. Well, how was it?"

"It was great. I would like to see her again the next time I am passing through," replied Buck.

"You act like you have never had a piece of ass before. She is a hooker and makes all her paid customers feel good."

Buck said, "Yes I have, I have had plenty. But this girl was real nice. She told me she was only working to save up enough money to pay her way through nursing school in the fall."

"And you believed that line? Boy, are you a piece of work. You really have a lot to learn, I don't know if you can make it out her on the road." John said to Buck as he was cranking up the truck.

"I believed her; this girl did not have any tattoos and was not into anything kinky. I really think I could have a relationship with this girl. You were not there and you do not know."

Big John said, "I did not have to be there, I have been there plenty of times and you cannot believe everything you are told especially not by a hooker. At any rate, how about checking our fuel route to Carson City in the Qualcomm? I think we need to get to 395 south."

From the passenger seat, Buck reached down and picked up the Qualcomm and checked the designated fuel route. It did say 395 south. "Yea, we do need to get to 395 south," said Buck.

"Check the computer for directions to the shipper if you don't mind," said John. Buck got the directions off the Qualcomm and recited them to John as he drove down 395. About thirty minutes later John pulled the rig into the Utility Trailer Manufacturing plant in Carson City. They checked in with the shipping department and John backed the rig into a vacant loading dock. They picked up a load of trailer parts and were scheduled to deliver it to Salt Lake City, Nevada by 0800 the next morning. Buck and John both rested in the sleeper in their respective bunks until they were loaded. It was Buck's turn to drive when the trailer was loaded. Buck climbed down from his upper bunk when the shipper came across the CB and informed them the trailer was ready to go. Buck went back to the loading dock and got their shipping manifest. He then went back tractor and climbed into the driver's seat. He had checked his route and he knew where he was going. He typed his loaded call into the Qualcomm and cranked the truck up and took off. John was sleeping in the sleeper. Buck had been doing a lot of the night driving. They were trying to work 12 hour shifts with one in the sleeper and one on duty. John had been driving during the day and Buck was catching the night shift.

Buck turned on the CB and keyed up the mike, "Break 19 for a west bound. Has that accident been cleaned up at mile marker 150 before you get into Winnemucca?" He got a quick response from a driver saying, "It was clear when I came through about 20 minutes ago. You got clear sailing all the way into Salt Lake City. Keep the hammer down. I have not seen the first Bear (affectionate term truckers use for highway patrolmen). What did you leave behind you? Over."

"I appreciate the comeback," said Buck, "I am afraid I cannot help you very much." I just jumped on 80 at Carson City. A driver back in Reno had told me there was a bad accident at the 150 yardstick and there was a big back up, so I just wanted to see if I needed to try to go around it or anything. Over."

"Naw, you won't have any problem," said the westbound driver. "It has all been cleaned up. You have yourself a safe trip. Over'"

"You too driver," said Buck, "This is *Rumblestrip*, I am eastbound and down, maybe I will catch you on the flipside." Buck turned down the CB and turned up the radio and cruised on down the highway. He rolled into his load destination about 0600 well ahead of schedule and checked in with the receiving department. It was a scheduled drop and hook stop, which meant that Buck would be dropping his loaded trailer and hooking to another loaded trailer.

So Buck put his load where he was told and went around the Warehouse and hooked to his new load, which they were taking to Seattle, Washington. When Buck got back from securing the load and hooking the glad hands (connectors) on the air lines and electrical cables to the new load, he saw John's head sticking out from the curtain which separated the sleeper area from the truck cab area. John said, "I did your empty call and your loaded call in the Qualcomm, so we are ready to go. Head up I-84 to yardstick 351. There is a Sapp Brothers truck stop there. We can stop for breakfast and I will drive from there."

Buck drove to the truck stop in short order. They were in need of fuel, so he pulled up to the fuel pumps and got out and filled up both tanks. Each tank held 150 gallons. Buck put almost 200 gallons in the tanks. The rig only got about 5-6 miles per gallon, so they were fuelling up about once a day.

After fueling up, Buck drove around the parking lot looking for an easy parking spot. The truck stop was huge. It must have held about 100 trucks and it was almost full. Buck found a parking spot at the back of the parking lot and it was easy to get the rig into it. Buck had already decided the hardest part of trucking was parking in a full truck stop. There were times when he would pull through a truck stop and if he did not see an easy place to park he would just keep on going to another truck stop. He had learned a lesson at a truck stop when he watched another driver back into a spot and knock the mirror of the truck in the space beside him. The driver came out of the truck that he hit and was fighting mad. He was an owner-operator and took a lot of pride in keeping his truck looking good and he was not happy that the inexperienced driver damaged his rig. He called the police had them wrote an accident report. I am sure that he got his damaged mirror fixed with insurance money from the other truck. Buck was very careful any time he was behind the wheel but he was especially alert in a full truck stop. They ate breakfast and since they got a free shower with a fuel up, they both took a shower at the truck stop. Sometimes it was difficult to do, but Buck tried to get a shower every day. He liked keeping himself clean. If he could not get a shower, he would always find a sink, wash his face, brush his teeth and, shave.

"Why didn't you park a little closer to the truck stop?" John said as they were walking back to the truck.

"Come on John, we need a little exercise, and it was an easy parking space."

"I guess you are right. You don't get a lot of exercise when you drive 10-11 hours a day, and sleep the rest of the time. It will be different when you get your own truck and you have to stop for a 10 hour break. You will have to do that to keep legal with your log book according to the FMCSA (Federal Motor Carrier Safety Act). You can make a little time for some exercise if you want."

"Yea I miss being able to work out. Before I started driving, I was going to the gym 3-4 times a week. I was in really good shape. I will have to figure out some way to keep in shape. I will walk, jog, or you know what is really good exercise – jumping rope. I need to put my jump rope on the truck. I would hate to get jumped by some smart assed driver and not be in shape to whip his ass." Buck had served three years in the marines, and was in good shape when he got out and he continued to keep himself in shape.

John and Buck made it back to the truck, climbed in, and filled out their log books for the previous day. Buck crawled back into the sleeper and was ready to catch up on his sleep. John cranked up the rig, jammed it into gear and they were on their way to Seattle.

Buck had been in the sleeper several hours when he felt the truck come to a stop. Buck usually woke up when the truck stopped. It meant there was a "pee" break and he usually needed one. When he got out of the sleeper, he saw a unique waterfall. John said, "Look at that! It is called sliding board falls."

"Let me get my camera out. I want a picture of that," said Buck.

John stopped the rig in Baker City and got some fuel and something to eat. It was Buck's turn to drive. It was about 1900 hours when Buck got under the steering wheel. John said, "Buck, you take it easy. You will be going down a steep mountain up the road. It is called *Dead Man's Pass* because there have been a lot of trucks go off the side of the mountain. The road does not have a guard rail. Just gear it down before you start down the mountain and you will be all right."

"What gear do you think I should be in?"

"Probably with our load, that Cummings engine will hold your speed down in seventh gear if you have got the Jake brake on. Whatever gear you get it in, once you start down the mountain, do not take it out of gear. That is when drivers get there ass in trouble. They knock it out of gear and when they get to going too fast, they can't get it back in gear and they ride the brakes until they get hot and crystallize and they can't stop the truck. Either that, or they lose air pressure and they do not have any air brakes." John could see the worried look on the rookie driver's face. "Don't get nervous. Just put it in seventh gear before you top the hill and leave it there as you start down the hill. You will be fine. Don't ride the brakes and don't pump them. Use stab braking and do not let the truck get above 50 mph. Do you know what stab braking is?"

"Yea that is what we were taught in truck driving school."

"Well, do it. My ass is in this truck too and I do not want to go flying off the mountain. Wake me up and I will drive down the mountain if you are too scared."

"I grew up driving in the mountains. I can handle it. You go ahead and get some sleep and I will get us to Seattle." Buck was not about to admit he was scared even though he was a little concerned about *Dead Man's Pass*. He had seen pictures of trucks that had lost their brakes and crashed coming down a mountain. He had also seen a number of trucks that had to hit the runaway truck ramps because they lost their brakes, and that did not look like too much fun either. It was bound to damage John's new Kenworth and you had to have a wrecker come pull you out of the sand in the runaway truck ramps. Buck did not want to be involved in either one of those scenarios.

Buck found a found a country music radio station and turned it up. John had lain down in the sleeper and Buck knew he would be asleep in short order. Buck had the volume on the CB turned down where he could hear it but did not drown out the radio. He was listening to a conversation on Channel 19 between two drivers. "How far is it to Tacoma?" said the one driver.

"It is about 320 miles," the CB crackled in a female voice. "You can get there in about 8 hours. You have a safe trip into Tacoma. You ought to be there by about 6 o'clock in the morning."

"I appreciate the comeback. I go by *Texas Pete*, what is your handle?"
"They call me *Songbird*."

"*Songbird*, I like that. It suits you. I got a telephone call; I'll talk to you later."

Now that Buck had a chance to talk, he keyed up his mike and said, "How about you *Songbird*? Have you got a copy on this weak radio?" "Yea, I got you, go come on back."

"How far up the road is *Dead Man's Pass*?"

"Oh, you got about 20-25 more miles. You got to climb up to the top of the mountain and then start down the other side. That is what they call *Deadman's Pass*. It is really not that bad. Just gear your rig down about two gears and take your time. It is only about 5-6 miles to the bottom of the mountain. It is only bad when there is a lot of fog or snow and ice. I go this way a lot and sometimes it is rough. This is a clear night. You won't have any trouble."

"10-4 Songbird, this is my first time on this road and someone told me about *Deadman's Pass*, and it sounds pretty bad. I came across the twins in Wyoming a couple of days ago and they weren't that bad. I have driven a lot of mountain roads, and I have never had a problem. I don't really want to start tonight. Do you know what I mean?"

"Yea, I know what you mean. I got to go that way too and I don't want any problems either. How long have you been driving?"

"I am in my second week of training with Whiteline. I have got 5 more weeks to go." "10-4, "I remember going through it. I was training with Whiteline three and a half years ago. I had a real good trainer. I still talk to her from time to time. She taught me lot. I stayed with Whiteline for two years and then I got my own truck. Now I drive this reefer for Westar. I am home every day and driving every night"

Texas Pete came back on the CB, "You guys are both a couple of rookies. Wait till you have been out here for 26 years like I have. Then you can call yourself a trucker. What is your handle Whiteline?"

"Rumblestrip"

"Rumblestrip, you be sure to keep your speed down on *Deadman's Pass.* There are some real *kiss your ass curves* on that road and if you go into them fast you can *kiss your ass goodbye. You would not be the first driver that did not make down that mountain. If you want to stay with Songbird and me, we are going that way. How much you got in the* box?"

"I got about 34,000 pounds according to my bills and we got good brakes. I think I will be all right. You guys will probably get out of my range pretty soon, we are governored to 68 miles per hour and you guys passed me like I was sitting still."

"We'll slow down of you want us to. We are not in that big of a hurry. We are both going to Tacoma and got plenty of time to get there. Don't we *Songbird*? Come on"

"10-4, we'll be your front door, back door or both if you want us to, *Rumblestrip* " "Thanks anyway, I think you are about out of my CB range already. Go ahead. Have yourself a safe one. I will catch you later. This is *Rumblestrip* signing off for now. I am northbound and down."

"10-4 *Rumblestrip,* maybe we will catch you on the flipside, says *Songbird.*"

"Yea, you take it easy down *Deadman's Pass* there *Rumblestrip*. I'll holler at you again," *Texas Pete* chimed in.

Buck settled down into driving up the mountain. It was a long curvy road going up the mountain. He had to gear the rig down to from 10th gear to 5th gear. To climb the steepest part and he watched his speedometer get down to 20 mph. Buck knew from experience that you should start down the other side in no more than I extra gear than it took to get up the mountain. So he had decided to put the rig in 6th gear to go down *Deadman's Pass.*

There was a mandatory truck information station that he had to pull into at the top of the mountain. Buck thought these stops were there to scare you real good before you wet down the mountain. There was a map of the mountain showing where the curves were and where the emergency *runaway truck ramps* were located. Buck pulled his rig into one of the parking spots and got out to make a quick check of the truck and trailer. He stopped behind the tractor where no one could see him and peed. Buck could not help but enjoy the crisp clean air. He took a deep breath filling his lungs with the air. He marveled in the fact that there could not be any pollution in this remote area and this high in elevation. He looked up at the clear sky and thought to himself that he had never seen so many stars out. It was as if all he had to do was reach up and he could touch the sky.

Buck checked out the information for truckers about the mountain and saw that there was only five miles to the bottom and the recommended speed for his load was 35 mph. He was ready to head down the mountain. John was sound asleep, so Buck did not wake him. The stop cleared his head and made him very alert as he started down the mountain. He got the rig up to 6th gear with the Jake Brake on and held it there. He could hear the engine revving up as it worked to keep the vehicle speed down. Buck watched his speed and used the stab braking technique to keep his speed no higher than 35 mph. When it got up to 35 mph, he would put on the brakes to get the speed back down to 30 mph and then let off. This technique kept the brakes from overheating.

Buck had gone about 1.5 miles down the mountain. He knew because he started at mile marker 263 and he was at 261.5. This was when he heard the low pressure alarm start going off. He looked down and saw the air pressure gauge was on 59 psi. Buck had no experience with this and this was John truck. Buck hollered back to John in the sleeper, "John! Wake up! We don't have any air pressure. " Buck watched his speed get up to 45 mph and he put on the brakes. They went almost to the floor and now Buck was really panicking.

John climbed up into the passenger seat when he heard the low pressure alarm going off, "What the hell is going on, Buck?"

"I don't know. Our air pressure is at 50 psi and dropping. We got 3 more miles to the bottom of the mountain."

"Well hang on; we are not going to be able to bring it to a stop. If we get too fast before that last curve, you will have to hit the ramp and we are not going to do that unless we have to," John said as he buckled his seat belt and watched the truck speedometer. It had gotten up to 45 mph and the sing for the curve up ahead was said 25 mph.

Buck was pushing on the brake pedal to get it to slow down. There weren't any other trucks on the road, so Buck was doing his best to straighten out the curves. He was still going into the curve way too fast. He hung on to the steering wheel and checked his mirrors to make sure the trailer was following his rig. The worst thing would be if the trailer started sliding and made them jack-knife as they were going through the curve. The curve was on the inside against some jagged rocks and they got dangerously close to the mountain as they listened to rocks and gravel flying as the skidded through the curve. Buck straightened it out as he came out of the curve and the road got a little straighter for a short distance before it entered and outside curve. If they were going too fast into the outside curve they would be hurtling off the mountain. There was no guard rail to stop them.

"Good job, Buck, hang on and keep braking. Stand up on that fucking brake if you have to. If the air pressure holds up, we will make it," screamed John. John was listening to the alarm, and watching the needle on the gauge. It was holding at 50 psi. Buck was slowing the rig down on the straight stretch. He managed to get the speed down to 40 mph and he could see the sign up ahead for the curve showing 20 mph. They were heading into the curve now and there was nothing they could do now but pray they would make it. Buck had a tight grip on the wheel and was up out of his seat pushing on the brake pedal. The rig was losing traction as it hit the shoulder and they were dangerously close to the cliff. The rig stayed true in the curve and started out the other end of the curve and the trailer miraculously followed the tractor through the curve. They had made it. They passed mile marker 58 and they had one more mile to go.

The runaway truck ramp was ahead and one last curve. They were travelling at 50 mph. The air pressure was still at 50 psi and the alarm had never stopped. The Jake brake was struggling to keep the speed down but it was not able to without the brake pedal.

Buck was still stepping on the brake and had very little pedal to work with. It was almost on the floor. It was slowing the rig down a little. As they got to the runaway truck ramp, the speed was down to 35 mph.

"Hang on Buck! You can make it! Get through this last curve and bring it to a stop and let's see what is wrong."

Buck guided it through the last curve and let it coast to a stop when the road straightened out and flattened out at the bottom of the mountain. The rig came to a stop right alongside mile marker 256. Buck set the parking brake and nearly collapsed in his seat. Meanwhile John got out and surveyed the rig. He saw what had happened. The trailer airlines were dragging the ground and one of them had developed a leak. That is what made the rig lose air pressure. John was wrapping the air hose with some duck tape when Buck came back to look under the trailer to see what John was doing.

"Did you check the airlines under the trailer before you started down the mountain?"

John asked Buck.

"Yea, I stopped at the pull-off at the top of the mountain and they were okay."

"Well, they must have come loose. They were dragging on the ground and one of them had gotten a leak. We were damn lucky that it wasn't any bigger. We would have lost all our air pressure and we could have kissed our ass goodbye up there on *Deadman's Pass*. You did a good piece of driving up there. I am not sure I could have held it in the road. If you have cleaned out your drawers, we will head on up the road. We will have to stop at the first truck stop with a repair shop and replace this bad hose, but I think it will be all right until then. Are you okay to drive?"

"Yea, I am still shaking. It scared the shit out of me. Let me go over here behind the bushes. I'll be ready to go in minute. I'll drive another hour and a half and then turn it over to you."

Buck drove up the straight road and came to a big truck stop in about an hour. The air pressure built up and stayed up the whole way. The duck tape must have worked. They put the rig in the shop and had them put on a new airline. All the big truckstops have shops to work on the big rigs. John and Buck went into the restaurant and got something to eat while the shop was working on the truck. When thy finished eating, they went back to the shop to see if the truck was ready. The shop was finished. John settled up with the shop for the repairs and then they hit the road again. John drove the rig into Seattle.

After they got unloaded, the qualcomm indicated they were going to pick up a load in Lewiston, Idaho and delivering to Chicago, Illinois.

"We are going to be travelling through some real pretty country going up through the Clearwater River Park in Idaho and then across the Dakotas," explained John to Buck. "You might want to keep your camera handy. I'll be glad to stop a few times along the way."

"Thanks I have never been through here before. I'll keep my camera handy" said Buck as he crawled back in the sleeper.

Buck had been in the sleeper for several hours when he overheard John talking on the CB, "Hey, how about that Whiteline? Have you got your ears on? Come on"

"Yea, I got a copy on you," came back the reply over the CB from the slow moving rig. "I think I am about out of fuel. That is why I am driving so slow."

"Well if you are about out of fuel, you are in a world of shit. We just passed a sign that said the next fuel station was 39 miles away."

"No, I did not see that sign. Where was it?"

"It was about 3-4 miles back. We will follow you just in case you do run out." "Thanks, I know I cannot make it 39 more miles. I have been on empty for the last 20 miles or more. The gauge is way past empty."

They had not goner more than 5 miles when the CB crackled, "Well, that is it. I am out of gas."

"Pull in the scenic look out just ahead of you," replied John. Both rigs were able to pull into the scenic look out. They were parked side by side. The driver of the out of fuel truck got out of his rig and walked over to John who had also gotten out of his truck. "My name is John, Everybody Calls me *Big John*, said John as he stuck out his big hand.

"My name is Raphael," said the other driver. "I have only been driving solo for two weeks."

"How did you run out of fuel? You must have missed your fuel stop. Let me look at your Qualcomm and I will see if you had a fuel stop." Raphael handed John the Qualcomm and John told Raphael that he missed his fuel stop. He should have filled up in Lewiston, Idaho at our terminal. John went on to say, "Well you have got two choices. You can call *On Road Assistance* and wait here for them to bring it to you. It will probably take them about 3-4 hours. They will not be too happy about bringing fuel out to you. They kinda think drivers should be smart enough not to run out of fuel. Or we can siphon enough fuel out of our tanks to get you to Missoula. You can get fuel there on your comdata credit card.

Raphael replied, "I really cannot wait around here 3-4 hours. I am supposed to be in Billings tonight by 1800 hours."

"OK, do you have a siphon hose? I usually carry one in my belly bin, but I think I took it out last time I was home. I cleaned out my belly bin and I think the siphon hose is still sitting in my garage in Charlotte, NC."

"No, I do not have a siphon hose."

"Well, let me get some tools and we can take off your heater hose and use it. Buck, you can get that bucket and roll up a placard for a funnel. You can do the siphoning. I don't like to breathe the diesel fumes. OK?"

'Well, fuck you, John. I don't like to breathe diesel fumes either. But I will. I have siphoned enough gasoline for my lawnmower over the years to know how to do it without drinking any fuel."

The trio set to work. They unhooked the heater hose and siphoned out 7-8 gallons of fuel from John's rig and put it in Raphael's tractor. When they were through they replaced the heater hose and Raphael started his rig up to make sure it would crank. Then John grabbed a can of gojo hand cleaner and they all went down to the stream bank to clean themselves up. Buck was real impressed with how beautiful the river was and the entire Clearwater gorge.

Buck said, "Man, I bet there are some big trout in this river. This is a pure mountain stream if I have ever seen one. Hey, Raphael, where are you from? I am usually pretty good with accents, but I cannot make yours out."

Raphael says, "I am from Somalia originally. My family moved to Minnesota when I was a baby. There are a lot of people from Somalia near Minneapolis, Minnesota. I drive out of the Waukesha Terminal. Where are you from?"

Buck answered, "I am from Rock Hill, SC. I am out of the Charlotte terminal. John here lives in Concord, NC. The home of NASCAR. So don't ask him about who he thinks will win the race Sunday in Charlotte. I will go ahead and tell you or you might not ever make it to Billings today. He thinks Jimmy Johnson will win it. I kind of like Jeff Gordon's chances myself."

"You wanna put some money on that, Buck? Put your money where your fucking mouth is. I'll tell you what. Let's just bet on which one finishes higher in the race. Let's put $20 on it to make it interesting, OK?"

OK, John, but I don't really want to take your money. You got all those mouths to feed you know and I don't."

"You don't worry about the money. I make enough to cover the $20 bucks if I lose."

John, Buck and Raphael headed back to their trucks. Raphael thanked them over and over for helping him out. John told Raphael to keep his CB on and we would follow him to the nearest truck stop. We would make sure he got some fuel and John would let him pay him back for the fuel we gave him.

John and Buck followed Raphael the 40 or so miles to a truck stop located right at I-90 in Missoula. John pulled his rig into the fuel island right beside Raphael. John pumped 8 gallons of fuel from the hose that Raphael was using the company credit card on and then gave it back to Raphael for him to fill his tanks. John was an owner operator and he had to pay for his fuel so it was only fair for Raphael to replace the fuel John had given him. Raphael headed for Billings and John and

Buck headed toward the truck stop to get something to eat after they had filled the fuel tanks.

As they were headed into the truck stop, there was a little blond headed girl sitting on the wall outside the entrance. She said to Buck when he got close enough, "Hey cutie, would you like some company tonight?"

John looked at Buck saw the eagerness on his face. Before Buck could answer the girl, John said, "No mam, he does not have time for any company tonight. We have got to leave for Chicago as soon as we get a bite to eat." After they got inside, John said, "You better be careful when you get on your own. You will spend every penny you make on *lot lizards* if you are not careful. That girl would have crawled up in my sleeper with you and given you whatever you wanted if you were willing to pay her for it. She might have given you more than you asked for. She might have given you something you can't get rid of."

"'You don't know. She looked like a pretty nice girl. She might have given it to me for free. I always use a rubber anyway. I am real careful with my private parts. You could have let me talk to her. You are not my fucking daddy, you know."

"Oh she was a crack whore. Trust me. Quite frankly I did not want her in my truck messing up my mattress or stinking up the inside of my truck. You don't know who she has been with. Besides, we are behind on our schedule since we spent so much time helping Raphael."

"I'll tell you one thing Raphael did for me. I gave me confidence. If Whiteline would give him a truck to haul freight, as dumb as he is, I know I can handle the job."

"You have still got a lot more to learn both on the road and off the road before you are ready for your own truck. I have been driving for 14 years and I learn something new every day. I would not get so cocky if I were you. I also might add that it is up to me, so you better pay attention these next four weeks or so. I can put you on a bus back to

South Carolina anytime I want to. I have done it before with trainees I thought could not make a driver or would not listen to me. I can also tell them you are not finished with your training. They want drivers, so they want you to finish in 7 weeks, but if I tell them you are not ready, it can take longer. You need to get better at backing and you need to be able to follow the directions to a site without getting lost. You have not found a pick-up or delivery site on your own yet."

"OK, I know, I know, I'll get better. But Raphael did convince me that if he can drive a truck, I know I can.

After they finished eating, Buck got back on the truck in the driver's seat and John crawled back in the sleeper. Buck checked his map real quick, filled out his logbook, cranked up the Kenworth and drove out of the truck stop and was on his way to Chicago. He figured he would probably need a power nap about 2-3 in the morning or he would get real sleepy tonight. He did not get much sleep during the day because they were busy helping Raphael out. Buck did not take any kind of stay awake pills. If he got tired while driving, he would pull into a rest stop or off ramp and take a nap. He had made a promise to himself before he started driving a truck not to sacrifice his health or his safety.

Buck turned on the CB and was listening to two truckers yapping about getting home to see their wife and eating some good home cooking. They were wanting some cornbread, pinto beans, fried chicken, and banana pudding. They could make a man hungry just talking about how good it was going to be. Buck was looking forward to getting home for the weekend and see his new girlfriend. He had already called her and told her he would be home on Saturday unless something went wrong, and he wanted to see her. She had agreed to see him on Saturday night. She said her roommate would be gone for the weekend and they could have the placed to themselves. Buck was horny and really looking forward to it. After they delivered this load to Chicago on Friday they should get a load to put them in Charlotte for the weekend. They had been gone for three weeks and it was time to route them back home for a few days. John normally ran three weeks out before he came for a three day weekend.

Buck had dated Lucy in high school and he ran into her at the grocery store in Rock Hill right before he started driving a truck. He had not gotten past first base with her when he dated her in high school and was quite surprised when, after three dates, she invited him in to her apartment and they made mad passionate love to each other. Buck was anxious to see her again when he got home.

Buck was right about needing a power nap about 0230. He started feeling a little sleepy and he pulled into arrest area and parked the rig in a vacant parking space. He crawled back into the upper berth of the sleeper and went to sleep for about 25-30 minutes. Buck had learned that he was much better off to go ahead and take a nap if he got sleepy than to fight it and keep driving. He had driven 12 straight hours one night and had actually had to douse water in his face to keep himself awake. He had heard too many stories about drivers that had gone to sleep behind the wheel and he decided that he should not take a chance. The rig and the load might be worth a million dollars or more, and his own life was priceless. So it was just too important to risk driving if he felt fatigued. He had learned that everybody had a circadian cycle that dictated when the body wanted rest and that everybody's cycle was different. That is why some people can work better at night and some people were better in the morning and so forth. Buck had come to realize that his body wanted rest around 0200-0300 and also around 1500-1600 hours. He had learned that the best thing to do when the body wanted rest was to give in to it and not fight it. It worked out a lot better that way. He had also learned that he could take a short nap and get up and drive and be alert.

Buck got up from his short nap and drove the rest of his shift and pulled into a truckstop around 0730 on Thursday morning. It was a scheduled fuel stop and he planned to get a shower, eat breakfast, and crawl into the sleeper berth and let John drive a while.

The rest of the week worked out very well. They got their load into Chicago late that afternoon. They picked up a loaded trailer in Gary, Indiana and took it to Columbus. Ohio. They dropped that trailer at a Sears distribution center. Then it was back to the Whiteline terminal in Columbus to pick up a loaded trailer and drop it at the Charlotte terminal. It all worked out and John and Buck rolled into the Charlotte terminal at1400 hours on Friday afternoon. John set their ETA for Monday morning at 1000 hours and told Buck to have a good weekend. Buck got his car and left for Rock Hill and John got his car and left for Concord.

When they got back to the tractor on Monday morning, they went into the terminal and checked with their Driver Managers to see what load they had on their truck. Buck's Driver Manager was a cute brown haired girl named Vickie, who was in charge of all the trainees in the Charlotte terminal. John's Driver Manager was a short stocky ex truck driver named Bill. Bill was a good guy with 4 years experience as a Driver Manager. Bill was good at keeping John's rig rolling and since John got paid by the mile, it was very important to keep those wheels turning. Bill told John that he knew that Buck was only a trainee, but he could tell Buck could do the job and he would run us like any other team drivers. He told John that he had a load picking up in Charlotte and headed for Denver, Colorado.

John and Buck got in their tractor, found an empty trailer to pull to the site so they could drop an empty and pickup a full trailer if tires bound for Denver, Colorado. After they got rolling Buck asked John, "Did you have a good weekend?"

"Yea I spend time with the wife and kids. It was a good restful weekend. Everything was good except the race. I guess you saw that your man Jeff Gordon won the race. Here is your $20 bucks", John said as he reached in his pocket and pulled out a twenty dollar bill from his wallet.

"Listen John, I don't want any hard feelings about this. I only bet you to make the race a little more interesting. I would rather you keep the money if you are going to have any hard feelings about it."

"Naw, it is OK, I'll get it back on the next race. We will bet the same thing on the race next week in Daytona if you want to. It kept my interest in the race. I watched the race and Jimmy Johnson would have won if he had not gotten in that mix up in turn 4 on lap 200 with Tony Stewart. He was leading the race up to that time. That opened the door for Gordon to cruise across the finish line. I still think Johnson had the fastest car and would have won if he had not got knocked into the wall. He will be back next week. How was your weekend?"

"Oh, you would not have believed it. It was great. When I got home, I dropped my clothes off with my Mom to wash and went with a friend of mine to a biker bar in Charlotte. He had just gotten a new Harley. It was nice. It is one of those new sotftail bikes. It made my old Kawasaki crotch rocket look pretty bad. But I got hooked up with a biker chick. We went to a motel and she did things to me I have never had done to me before. She went into the bathroom when we got there. And when she came out, she only had her chaps on and damn she looked hot. She came over to me and peeled my clothes off. She gave me a blow job that was unbelievable. This girl really knew how to suck a dick. I believe she could have sucked the chrome off a trailer hitch. Anyway she got me off real quick. I shot off all over her face and she loved it. She licked the cum off and swallowed it. She said she loved the taste of cum."

"She let me know real quick that she was not through with me. She squeezed my dick and got it real hard again. Then she got on the bed on all fours and told me to fuck her. I put on a rubber and crawled up behind her and socked it to her. The harder I fucked her the more she liked it. She got real excited and begged me to spank her. I was hesitant at first because I did not want to hurt her. But she kept begging me to spank her harder. The harder I spanked her, the more excited she got. She screamed out when she came and gushed her cum all over me. I have never had a girl cum like that before. She was real wet. She rolled over on her back and pulled me on top of her. We fucked every way you could do it. I came three times and she must have cum 12-13 times. I lost count. She kept saying over and over that she loved my big dick. I left that motel and I could hardly walk. I went home. I had to get some rest. I had a date Saturday night with a girl that I have been seeing and I knew I would need my strength for her."

John said, "So you got yourself a hold of a real gusher, Huh?

"Yea, you would not have believed it. There was a big wet spot on the sheet when we got through. It was about this big," Buck said as he made a big circle with his hands and arms.

"Anyway, Saturday afternoon, I went over to my girlfriend, Lucy's apartment, and she made me supper and we went to bed after that and made love. It was real slow and gentle and felt real good. It was completely different from the night before with the biker chick. Lucy likes it slow and easy and wants me to whisper sweet nothings in her ear while we are fucking. She will squeeze me real tight and hold me deep inside her when she cums. She really likes it when we have mutual climaxes."

"You better watch out for that one if you want to stay single. She sounds like the marrying kind," said John.

'Oh I am sure she would marry me. But I think she would want me to come off the road. I can't do that right now. Maybe after a couple of years over the road, I could get a job that would get me home every night. I might consider settling down then. I am not sure about Lucy though. She seems to have a problem with credit cards. She likes to use that plastic money and does not seem to realize she has to pay them off. I think she has run up about $6,000 -$7,000 on several cards and has trouble making the payments. I answered the phone one time and it was Macy's saying she was late with her payment. I don't need that. I use a credit card, but I make sure I pay it off every month. I don't like those 18% interest charges or those $29 late payment charges."

"I tore up all my wife's credit cards. She would run them up to the maximum and make minimum payment. We were paying $300 a month in interest and late payment charges. That is crazy. I got them paid off and we don't use them anymore. If you do not have the money to buy something, then you don't need it is my philosophy."

Buck and John rode together for four more weeks of training. Buck learned a lot from John. John had taught Buck how to slide the trailer tandem axle to balance a load so that it was legal when you went across a DOT scale. Buck had learned how to keep his DOT log book legal and how to be safe on the road. Those were the things that got you in trouble with the safety officers of Whiteline and would get you fired if you could not keep yourself legal and safe.

Buck became much better at backing and following directions so he did not miss turns or get lost. Buck was ready after his six weeks of training to get his own truck and drive solo. He and John got along fine, but that tractor could get pretty small at times when you had two people on the truck and all their food and gear for three weeks on the road. It was also hard to get a good 7-8 hours sleep with the truck rolling. There was a lot of stopping and starting to load and unload and with traffic back ups. And more than once, John had stomped on the brakes pretty hard and rolled Buck out of the sleeper into the floor of the tractor.

Chapter Three

Buck was excited and a little frightened when he arrived at the terminal in Charlotte to be issued a truck and get his first load to drive solo. He really hoped it would not be a long run. A lot of things could happen on the road and most of were not good. The only thing you wanted to happen was to pick up the load on schedule and deliver it in good shape on schedule. Buck checked in with his driver manager and was given the keys to his first tractor. He went out to the yard and found it in line with several other tractors. It was a Freightliner, over two years old with 450,000 miles on the speedometer. Buck gave the outside a walk around inspection. He did not see anything major wrong with the outside of the tractor. There were a couple of scratches on the fenders. He made note of them on inspection sheet he was given when a tractor was assigned to a new driver. He opened the hood and checked the engine and all the visible parts under the hood. He checked out the belly bin of the tractor and saw that it had a fully charged fire extinguisher, some load straps, and some emergency triangle for parking on the road in an emergency. He climbed inside the cab. He checked out the radio and the CB. They both worked fine. He checked out the sleeper area and all the compartments. The previous driver had done a good job of cleaning out their personal items. All that was left in the cab of the tractor were the registration papers for the truck and all the permits needed to haul freight in all 48 states of the USA and some company forms and manuals.

Buck cranked the tractor up and listened to the engine. He opened the hood and checked out the engine for anything obvious. The engine sounded fine and most tractors were good for close to a million miles before the company got rid of them. Buck would have liked to have gotten one of the new Volvos that the company was getting, but he realized that he would have to start out with an older truck and prove himself a good driver to the company before they would put him in a new truck. He drove the tractor around the yard and then went inside to tell his driver manager that he would let them issue him the truck. Buck's driver manager made the necessary entries into the computer and told him he would be assigned a load probably within the next hour.

Buck drove his newly assigned tractor up the road to the truck stop so he could get used to it and to check it out before he went on the road with it. It would be better to find out any problems before he was on the road with it for two to three weeks. He went inside the truck stop and got him a quick lunch at the buffet. He got back on his truck after eating. His on board Qualcomm was blinking that he had a message. He checked his load assignment and discovered he had been assigned a load of tires going from Charlotte to Detroit, Michigan. Buck went back to the terminal, hooked to an empty trailer, accepted his load assignment and filled up his fuel tanks. By this time his tractor had been dispatched. He needed to pick up his load within the next 3 hours.

Buck's trip to Michigan went without a hitch. He delivered his load of tires on schedule and got some confidence in himself that he might really be a truck driver. Buck was beginning to realize that his company, Whiteline, did not get a lot of respect from other drivers on the road. All the company trucks were governored to 65 mph and we could become rolling road blocks to other trucks behind us that wanted to go faster. Most of the owner operator trucks did not have governors and they could go as fast as you would let them. Even the Whiteline owner operator trucks like the one Buck trained on were governored at 70 mph. Additionally Whiteline hired new inexperienced drivers, some of which were accident prone. Buck listened to a lot of trash talk on his CB about Whiteline drivers.

Buck was in the center lane of a three lane road in Atlanta when a big green Peterbilt rig got right on his bumper. Buck heard a deep voice come over the CB saying, "Just wanted to let all you drivers out there know there is a big chunk of scrap metal in the middle of the center lane heading south on 85 at yardstick number 88. Oh my bad, that is a Whiteline truck."

Buck realizing that the driver was referring to his truck came back, "Look ass wipe, I don't know what your problem is but I am quite happy here in the centerlane. Whiteline pays road taxes and there is no law saying I cannot drive in this lane if I want to. Besides, it is safer here than in the inside lane where all the traffic is merging on and off the expressway. There are three lanes out here pick one and go on down the road. I am not slowing you down. And get off my ass! If you want to pull that rig over, I'll kick your ass."

"The driver behind Buck came back on his CB, "I'd like to see you try. If the traffic was not so heavy, I'd gladly pull over and we would see who would kick whose ass. You don't sound like a very big guy to me."

"I am big enough to back up what I am telling you," replied Buck. "I think you are a lot of mouth myself."

About that time the big green Peterbilt came out from behind Buck on his outside lane and began to pull up beside him. The driver got even with Buck's rig and Buck saw that he was a burly man about 35 with a full beard, no shirt sleeves, and a lot of tattoos. "Get a good look, Boy. I hope I will see you again when I will have a chance to teach you a thing or two." The driver sped on past Buck shooting him a bird as he went by. The Peterbilt eased over into Bucks lane and Buck had to slide his rig over into the inside lane to get out of his way. Buck got real close to a car beside him and it had to move over a bit also.

"Hey Fuckface," says Buck, "You almost took my front bumper off. You don't scare me. You better hope you do not see me again. I will remember you and your rig and I will kick your ass. That is not a threat! That is a promise."

"Fuck you, the only thing you will see on me is my rear taillights. All you slow assed Whiteline drivers are alike. You are always in the way. You do not seem to realize we are paid by the mile and you cost us money when we get stuck behind you and your slow assed trucks."

The green Peterbilt was not governored and it sped on out of sight. Buck watched it go down the road and vowed to get even with the driver for running him off the road. Buck turned his radio to a slow jazz station. That always calmed him down in traffic. It was hard to get road rage when you were listening to Kenny G.

Buck was traveling down I-75 south of Atlanta and saw a billboard advertising an oriental health spa with plenty of truck parking. He decided he needed a break and a good relaxing massage might be just the thing he needed. He pulled his rig into the parking lot, set the brake and went inside the building not quite knowing what to expect. In a few seconds a very attractive young oriental girl opens the door and asks Buck if he would like a massage.

Buck checks the girl out and says, "Well I am not sure. What does a massage costs?"

The petite good looking young oriental girl replied. "It is $40 for a half an hour or $75 for an hour."

Buck said, "I think a half an hour will be enough." Buck shelled out $40 and handed it to young girl. She took the money and grabbed Buck's hand and led him back to a small room with a massage table. She told him to take off his clothes and she would return in a minute. Buck was not sure what was in store for him, but he was not shy, so he took off his clothes and wrapped towel that was lying on the massage table around him. The pretty young oriental girl said to Buck, "My name is Judy. We need to get you cleaned up. Come with me."

Judy grabbed Buck's hand and led him back to a room with a shower stall and a hand washing wand. She told Buck to lie on the table and she proceeded to wash him off with the wand. She washed him of real good and spent more than a little time washing his 8.5" hardon. Judy commented that he had a large dick.

When Judy was satisfied that Buck was clean, she lead him back to the little massage room and told him to lie on his stomach. Buck climbed up on the massage table and placed the towel over his butt. Judy started massaging his feet and gradually worked her way up his body. Buck was really enjoying Judy's soft hands. He was getting real relaxed. Judy worked her way up his back side and really gave his shoulders and arms a good rubdown. Buck was feeling real relaxed and was enjoying looking at Judy in her oriental bikini top outfit. Judy told Buck to turn over and she would do his front. Buck rolled over and he still had the towel covering his private parts. It was very obvious that he still had his hardon. Judy had a way a lingering around that area of his body while she was giving him his massage so between her skimpy outfit and her lingering soft hands around his groan area, Buck had never lost his hardon. Judy massaged his frontal area and she was getting more obvious about paying attention to his groan area. She lightly glided her finger over his abdomen and pushed his towel down so that his 8.5" dick was standing straight up. She lightly rubbed up and down on the shaft.

She said to Buck, "Your time is about up would you like me to continue to massage you as she was grabbing and rubbing his shaft up and down."

Buck replied, "Yea, don't stop now. It feels too good"

Judy replied, "I can finish you with this" and she held out her hands. "Or I could finish you with this," and she pointed to her mouth. "Or I can finish you with this," and she pointed to her pussy. "It depends on how much you want to tip me. $50 for this," as she held out her hands.

$100 dollars for this," and she pointed to her mouth. "$150 for this," and she pointed to her pussy. "Or $250 for all three." She said first you have to pay another $50 for an extra half an hour. I have to pay my boss.

Buck said, "I want the full treatment. I want the works." Buck shelled out 3 one hundred dollar bills and gave them to Judy. She took the money and headed out of the room. She told Buck she would be right back.

Judy returned shortly and said to Buck, "You just lay back Truck Driver and let Judy take care of you." Judy proceeded to do just that. She took off all her clothes and gave Buck a real good look at her. Buck admired her body. She had full round tits and a firm round ass. She had just enough pubic hair to make her pussy very inviting. "You like, Truck Driver???" Judy said. Buck replied as he could barely speak the words his desire and anticipation was at such a high level, "Oh, I like very much. You are beautiful."

Judy walked up beside Buck ad gently grabbed his dick. It responded very quickly to her touch. Judy started jacking his dick up and down. The she bent over and put the tip of his dick in her mouth. Buck was wild with desire. He was afraid he would cum too soon. He was trying to take his mind off the good feeling he was getting from having her mouth on his dick. She was bobbing her head up and down on his shaft. It was too big for her to go all the way down on it. But she was trying to get the whole 8 1/2 inches down her throat. Buck was "bucking" his body up and down on the table. Judy got him almost to the point of no return and then she stopped. Buck was going crazy. He thought she was going to ask for more money and at this point he would have given her all he had to finish him off. Buck looked own and she was removing a rubber from its package and placing it on the head of his dick. After she had stretched it down on the head of his dick she gently rolled it down the shaft. It was a tight fit and it was difficult to get it on.

Buck helped her with the last little stretch so that it would be tight on his shaft.

Judy climbed up on top of Buck and slid his massive boner up into her tight pussy. Buck felt the tightness of her pussy around his shaft and thought he was going to explode. Judy said, "How do you like that Truck Driver?"

Buck replied, "Oh my God, that feels good. Keep fucking me, Judy."

Buck knew he was getting close. He knew he would not last much longer. Judy was fucking him up and down with a steady rhythm now. Buck could not hold out much longer. Buck said, Judy, I am about to cum, How about finishing me off with your mouth and let me take this rubber off?" "Okay Truck Driver," Judy replied. Judy pulled her pussy up and away from Bucks dick. She then kneeled down in between his legs and grabbed the shaft of his dick. She stuck it in her mouth and began stroking and fucking his dick with her hand and mouth. Buck knew the time was near. He could not help himself. He screamed out, "I am cumming. Oh God, I am cumming" Buck shot wads of cum up from his dick. Judy held his dick straight up and so she could watch how high it would go. The first spurt went maybe 6" in the air, but the second one went probably 3 feet and landed on Judy's stomach. The 3rd, 4th and fifth spurts were just as strong. They went about 3' in the air. Two of the spurts landed in Judy's hair. Buck must have squirted 9-10 times before he was through.

Buck lay back on the table and had never felt so relaxed. Judy said to Buck, "Did you have happy ending, Truck Driver?"

"Oh yea, I had a very happy ending. Couldn't you tell? God that was good."

You like to give Judy tip? Truck Driver?"

"Yea, here is $20 more, Buck said as he reached in his pants pocket for a $20 bill."

"Okay, Truck Driver, you lay there and relax. You can get up and put your clothes on when you get ready. Thank you very much. I am happy too because you are happy."

Buck went about his routine of picking up and delivering loads for several days. Nothing very eventful happened until one night Buck pulled into a truck stop outside of Indianapolis. The truck stop was pretty crowded. It was about 2100 hours when Buck pulled into the truck stop. He found a spot and backed his rig in real slow. He knew he was close to the trailer in the spot directly behind him, but the front of his rig was sticking out in the traffic lane. So he eased back and ever so softly his rig bumped the trailer behind him. Buck was still a little surprised because he looked at the rig on either side of his and the front end of his rig was sticking out in the traffic lane by about 10-12 feet. Buck got out of his rig and went to the back of his trailer to survey the situation. Before he got to the back of his rig, he could tell that the trailer behind him was 12-15 feet inside his lined off space, and that was the reason he could not back up far enough into his space.

When Buck got back to the back of his trailer the driver from the truck behind him was standing there and says to Buck, "What the fuck are you backing into my trailer for?" Buck looked at him and looked up to the front of the rig and recognized them both immediately. It was the green Peterbilt and the burly truck driver with a beard that had tried to run him off the road a few days ago. Buck did not think he recognized him.

Buck responded, "Look where you are parked. You are way a good fucking 10 feet over the line. My truck is sticking out in the traffic. Can you pull your rig up a little?"

"That still does not give you the right to back into my trailer," retorted the burly truck driver.

"I did not hurt your trailer. You have bumped docks a lot harder than I hit you. It did not hurt you trailer or mine, so don't get your bowels in such an uproar," said Buck.

Buck saw the driver ball up his fist as he said, "Well FUCK YOU! I think I ought to teach your little smartass a lesson in manners."

Buck said, "You do not want to fuck with me. But my ass is just like a salad patch. You can get a mess anytime you want to."

When Buck said that, he could see the burly man bringing up a big haymaker with his right arm. Buck's extensive boxing training took over and he brought up his guard in a boxing stance and blocked the punch with one hand and delivered a counter punch to the other driver's midsection. It felt like his fist went all the way through the fat belly to the driver's back bone. The driver doubled over and Buck had to lift his body back up with his knee to deliver an uppercut to the burly man's head. The punch landed right between the eyes and the driver fell backward like a board and landed flat on the pavement.

He was out cold. Buck was afraid he had killed him. He checked his pulse and there was a strong pulse. Buck breathed a sigh of relief. I guess some other driver had seen what was going on and had announced it over the CB, because several other drivers showed up to see what was going on. Buck told them "Take care of this man. I was going to spend the night here, but I can't get my rig in this parking space without the front end sticking out in traffic, so I think I will go on down the road."

One of the drivers replied, "I sure hope I am not ever in your parking space. It is not worth the ass whipping I just saw you give this man." The other drivers all laughed at that comment. Buck just smiled at them and said, "There was a little more to it than that, but let's just say he had it coming. Thank you for taking care of him."

With that Buck crawled back into this rig and drove down the expressway to the next truck stop down the interstate.

Chapter Four

Buck was headed down I-95 on his way back from Florida one Sunday morning and was listening to the radio play some good country music. He noticed a van pull off on the shoulder up ahead of him and saw a whole family of passengers bailing out of the van. Buck looked closer as the vehicle came into view and he noticed that the left rear wheel was on fire. Buck thought to himself, "This can't be good." Buck pulled over onto the side of the road on the shoulder just ahead of the vehicle. As he pulled to a stop he could see a teenaged black boy running to catch up with his rig. Before Buck could get out of the truck and get to his fire extinguisher, the boy was waiting there beside him. As soon as Buck could extract the extinguisher from the vehicle, the boy grabbed it out of his hands and sped off with it. He pulled the pin on the fire extinguisher and had the fire under control by the time Buck could get back to the vehicle.

The family was a well dressed black family that was apparently on their way to church. They all thanked Buck profusely for stopping to help them. Buck got his empty fire extinguisher back so it could be recharged when he got back to his terminal. He walked back to his rig and rolled on up the highway. That was not the end of his excitement that particular Sunday.

Buck heading north up through Georgia later that same day and he got a real show from a car passing his rig in the "hammer" lane. Buck had been flashed before by women in passing cars baring their breasts as they rode by, but he had never gotten a show like this. Usually the other trucks on the road will alert you way ahead of time when women are flashing truckers. Buck had his CB on when he heard a fellow driver key up his mike and say, "Whoa, check out the blue Honda SUV rolling north in the hammer lane at mile marker 29 she will give you a real "peekaboo". Buck was at mile marker 33 so he knew the blue SUV would come into view shortly. He started watching his rear view mirror. He could barely make out a blue vehicle that was just a speck in his mirror, but it was gaining on him. He kept watching his rear view mirror as it got closer. The vehicle was going a lot faster than Buck's truck and it caught up with him very quickly.

When the SUV was alongside Buck's driver side window, it slowed down and stayed right beside his truck. Buck could look down into the SUV's window and had a clear view of the inside of the vehicle. What Buck saw as he looked down into the vehicle beside him came as a real pleasant surprise. Buck could see very clearly inside the vehicle a girl sitting in the passenger seat with her pants pulled down around her ankles. She was wearing a pair of very sexy pink panties and the guy driving the vehicle was rubbing his hand in small circles around the crotch of the pink panties. Buck could not see the faces of the man or the woman in the SUV because of his viewing angle down into the car. He could tell the woman had a very good figure and good looking legs.

The vehicle stayed right beside Buck's rig and gave him a clear view for several minutes. Buck was disappointed when the SUV started going a little faster and moved on ahead of Buck's truck. Buck had it mashed to the floor, but he could not keep up with the vehicle because his truck was governored to a top speed of 65 mph. The vehicle moved out ahead of Buck and he could no longer see down into the SUV. Then to Buck's surprise he started gaining on the vehicle. It was slowing down. Buck caught up with the vehicle as it came back into his view. Buck could see down into the vehicle again as it stayed right beside his driver side window. The view was a little different this time. The woman had pulled the pink panties down around her ankles and Buck could clearly see a dark haired triangle of a bush. The woman had a good looking body and just the right amount of natural hair to decorate her pussy. Buck could clearly see that the guy driving the car had his hand on the woman's hairy pussy. He was pushing the tip of his finger in and out of her pussy.

Buck was getting pretty excited by this time. He had a raging hardon. Buck had to pull his massive boner out of his pants and stroke it a little. He watched the show several minutes as he stroked his 8.5" dick. Again the SUV sped off and went out of view. Buck was hoping the show was not over. Sure enough to Buck's delight, the vehicle slowed up and came back alongside his truck. This time Buck could not believe what he saw. The woman had turned around completely and spread her legs so that Buck had a clear view of her beautiful pussy. She was pushing a 6" vibrator in and out of her pussy and hunching her body up and down up toward the window. This went on for several minutes and Buck was really jacking his dick now. He knew he should not be doing this while he was driving, but he was at a point that he could not stop. Much to Buck's disappointment the vehicle sped up and this time it went out of site. Buck watched the vehicle speed off and realized the show was over. Buck was pretty worked up by this time so he pulled off the edge of the road at the next exit he came to and parked his rig. He crawled back into his sleeper and plugged in a porno movie into his DVD. He finished the job he had started while he was driving. It only took about one minute before his massive dick was squirting cum all over the place. Buck impressed himself with how high he could squirt his cum. The first squirt went way over his head and hit the sidewall of his vehicle. He would have to be more careful he thought to himself. He was not sure he could clean it all up. He felt cool, calm and relaxed as he lay there in his sleeper. He cleaned up his mess and then rolled over and took a short nap before he got up and continued on his way to Richmond, Virginia.

Buck thought he would spend the night near Charlotte, NC. He gave Lucy a call to see if she might be available tonight. Buck dialed the number and told Lucy he would be coming through Charlotte tonight on his way to Richmond, Virginia. Lucy sounded very glad to hear from him. They had not seen each for a couple of weeks. Buck had been on the road and he would not get back to his home for another week. He was scheduled to stay on his truck for three weeks before he would get a weekend off. Lucy explained to Buck that she wished he had called her earlier. She was at her Mother's house and would not be back until late that evening. Buck was obviously disappointed. He suggested that she come by his truck on her way home. He told her he could park in a vacant lot not too far from her house and he hoped she could come by and see him. Lucy allowed that she could probably get there by about 2130.

Buck said that would be fine. He thought he would get to the vacant lot just off the interstate near Charlotte, NC around 2100. He would be out of driving hours, so he would need to take a 10 hour break before he could start driving again. He told Lucy he would love to see her. They agreed to meet and they were both looking forward to the rendezvous.

Buck got to the exit with the vacant lot a little before 2030 hours. He called Lucy and told her he was at the exit and to make sure she knew where he was parked for the night. Lucy knew where the vacant lot was and she said she could be there in about 20 minutes. She explained she was just about to leave her Mother's house. There was a convenience store next to the vacant lot and Buck walked over to it and went to the bathroom. He had taken a shower at the truck stop he stayed at last night before he left this morning. He felt pretty clean, but he did wash his face, brush his teeth, and shave in the bathroom. He bought some crackers and tuna salad and a drink and went back to his truck. He put on a clean shirt and used deodorant and body powder liberally to all parts of his body in anticipation of Lucy joining him on his truck.

Buck turned on his TV and found that he could pick up a local station very clearly. He ate his tuna salad and crackers and was lying in his sleeper watching TV when he heard Lucy's car drive up beside the truck. Buck got up and crawled out of his rig to greet Lucy. She got out of her car and hugged Buck immediately. Buck said, "You look beautiful. I like those jeans and top. They look real good together and they show off your figure real well." Lucy beamed and said, "Thank you. You look real good to me too. I have been really wanting to see you again. I am so glad you called."

Buck said, "I will be home next weekend for three days and I was hoping to see you then. It just happened that I had this load coming through Charlotte today and decided to spend the night here. But this makes it real special being able to meet you here. I have been wanting to see you again ever since the last time we were together. Have you ever been in a big truck?"

"No, this is my first time," replied Lucy.

"Well, climb on board and welcome to my home on wheels," said Buck as he helped Lucy climb up into the passenger seat. Lucy was full of excitement and very interested in what everything was. Buck pointed to the CB and told her that that was how truckers communicate to each other on the road. Buck turned it on and keyed up his mike, "radio check, has anybody got a copy on my weak radio?" A driver came right back and said, Yea, I got you loud and clear. Go ahead."

Buck keyed his mike again, "Thanks for the comeback, driver. I got my girlfriend here and she wants to talk to you. She has never talked on a CB. What is your handle?" They call me *waterdog*. Put your girfriend on, I will talk to her" Buck watched her reaction when he called Lucy his girlfriend and he could tell she really liked it.

"Okay *Waterdog* my handle is *Rumblestrip*. Here is my girlfriend, Lucy." Buck handed the mike to Lucy and showed her how to key it up. Lucy keyed up the mike and said, "Hello"

The driver came right back and said, "Well hello, Lucy, you sound like a very attractive young lady. Have you ever been told that before?"

Lucy said, "Yea, I have had people tell me that?"

"10-4, Lucy, tell me something. Are you going to be good to *Rumblestrip* tonight?" Lucy beamed at Buck and said, "I am always good to *Rumblestrip*."

"10-4, us truck drivers work hard and we need special treatment when we come home. You know what I am saying?"

"I think I know what he needs and I plan to give it to him" again Lucy beamed at Buck. Buck smiled back at her.

The driver came back, "Your signal is getting weak so I am going to let you kids get to it. This is *Waterdog*, northbound and down. Have yourselves a good night and a good day tomorrow. Maybe I will catch you on the flipside."

Lucy keyed the mike and said, "10-4, *Waterdog*, I enjoyed talking to you."

Buck took the mike and said, "You have yourself a safe trip, *Waterdog*, I'll catch you out here again and give you a holler."

Buck told Lucy that the CB had kept him from getting stuck in a back up. Drivers had alerted him to an upcoming back-up and told him how to go around it on several occasions. It had also alerted him to road hazards. Just the other day there was a lawnmower lying in the granny lane and he moved over to the hammer lane to avoid it. That could have been a disaster if he had not been alerted in time.

Buck showed Lucy the truck controls, the gear shift, and then he told her he had a refrigerator and a TV / DVD player. I have all the comforts of home.

"Do you want to lay down in my sleeper and see how comfortable it is?" asked Buck

"Okay," said Lucy as she crawled back into the bottom bunk of the sleeper. "This is comfortable."

Buck said, "I am glad you like it," as he lay down beside her. They embraced in a passionate kiss and it was not long before they were trying to get each other's clothes off. The sleeper was barely long enough for Buck when he stretched out all the way and it was only as wide as a cot. But the couple managed to wiggle out of their clothes and were naked in the sleeper. Buck remembered how good the sex was the last time they were together and he did not want to rush. He climbed on top of Lucy and very gently slid the head of his dick into her pussy. "Gawd, that feels good. You are so wet, said Buck.

Lucy said, "Your dick feels wonderful in my pussy."

Buck said, "You tell me when you want a little more. I only put the head in and I am going to wait till you tell me you are ready for some more."

"I am ready, Lucy replied, "give me some more of that big dick."

Buck slid another couple of inches of his long dick into her. He could tell she was pushing her pussy up to him and that she wanted more. "I believe you were ready. Are you about ready for the whole thing?" Buck could feel her juices were flowing.

"God yea, Buck, Fuck me. I am going to cum," said Lucy. Buck slid his eight and a half inch dick all the way into her pussy for several thrusts then he pulled it out to where the head was all he was giving to her. "Fuck me, Buck. Don't stop," said Lucy. Buck slammed his dick into her repeatedly, and he could feel a warm gush of her love juices all over his dick. He liked it when she begged, but he knew he would not last much longer. He could feel he was about to cum.

"You are going to make me cum," Buck said and Lucy responded, "I am going to cum to." Buck kept on pumping and when their climaxes hit them, they both screamed out simultaneously, "Aaaaaaaaaaghhhh" in pure ecstasy.. They lay together naked in an embrace and enjoyed the afterglow of sex for a long time. They both dozed off in complete satisfaction.

Buck did not know how long he had slept, but when he awoke he gently grabbed Lucy's hand and placed it on his dick. It responded immediately to her touch. Lucy came out of her sleep a little groggy and realized that she was squeezing the shaft of Buck's dick he had a blue steel hardon. Lucy did not want to waste such a magnificent hardon and she got up on top of Buck and sat on his dick. She started out slow because his dick was so big, it took a little getting used to when she first put it in, but then she began a grinding back and forth rhythm with her pelvis. It was like their bodies knew exactly what o do to each other for the maximum amount of pleasure.

Buck exclaimed, "Gawd, Lucy, you are going to make me cum again."

Lucy said, "I want you to, I want all your cum. I want you to fill my pussy up. My pussy loves it when you cum."

"Here it cums, aaaaaaghhhh, said Buck. Lucy was cumming to. They could both feel their juices mix. When she rolled off Buck, they could feel a big wet spot under them. Buck looked at it and said, "Uh Oh, that will make a stain on the mattress if I don't clean it up." He got some cleaner out from his cabinet and got some water from his refrigerator and they cleaned it up as best they could. Lucy did not think it would leave a stain after they got through. Buck turned the mattress over and they put their clothes on. Lucy went on home. She would have spent the night on his truck but Buck said he had to leave early in the morning to keep on his schedule. He promised he would call her the next weekend when he was home for three days. She seemed happy about seeing him again. Buck really liked Lucy and he felt she really liked him even though they had not been together but twice.

Buck knew they were running him pretty hard and he was pleased with his abilities as a truck driver to get his loads delivered on time and in good shape. He had become an expert in backing his rig into tight places. The only thing he was still having trouble with was blind side backs, which were backs that his trailer was on his blind side or passenger side of his truck. When he had to perform a blind side back, he generally got help or would set his brake and get out and look. *GOAL* was a term that they used in truck driving school, it stood for Get Out And Look. Most accidents in a truck were when backing up and most could be avoided if the driver would get out and look before he backed into something.

Buck still missed some turns and sometimes the Qualcomm directions were not easy to follow. He hated it when that happened because it was extra time and unnecessary effort spent on a load, and it ended up costing him money. The trip only paid for a designated amount of miles and he did not get any extra pay for riding around lost or looking for a shipper or a consignee. He was getting a lot better at it and tried to plan his trip out before he started to avoid any problems. He also vowed he would put a GPS system in his truck to help him find places he had not been before. He knew he had to be careful with it though because if you followed it, it could put you on roads that were not made for trucks.

Buck had already had to stop at a fire department in New Jersey to get directions for getting his truck out of the area. He was delivering a load of computers to a warehouse near Hackensack, New Jersey. He missed a turn and instead of going east on US Highway 46, he was going west and he made three turns onto roads that had a low bridge. Buck, in desperation, stopped his truck on the side of the road at a fire department and asked how to get back on the interstate to get out of New Jersey. The fireman was very helpful and told him the way to get his big truck out of town. And Buck followed the directions explicitly because it was not the most direct route, but it was the safest, and it avoided all the low bridges.

Chapter Five

Buck was delivering a load of pallets to Birmingham, Alabama. He pulled into Birmingham at about 1800 hours the night before and he had a scheduled delivery at 0800 the next day. He found truck stop near his consignee and pulled his rig into the lot. As he was finishing backing into his parking spot a slender black man came up to his truck and said, "Hey driver, I am going to hook you up."

Buck replied, "What are you going to hook me up with?"

The black guy retorted, "What do you need? I got some good stuff to make you feel good or I can get you a good looking woman. Just tell me what you want." Buck said, "I don't do drugs, man. I am not interested in any of that."

Okay, says the black guy. "I'll send a girl over to talk to you. You will like her. She is good looking and can take good care of you."

Buck said "OK Bro, send her out to me I will talk to her. That may be all I do, but I will talk to her." Buck shut his truck off and filled out his log book. He thought to himself that maybe he would like some female companionship tonight.

Buck went inside the truck stop to go to the bathroom and get something to drink. He had some cheese and bologna in his refrigerator to make a sandwich out of on his truck. When he got back to his truck, there was an attractive young blond haired girl at his truck.

When Buck got close to her, she said, "Hi truck driver, my name is Cherry, do you want some company tonight." Buck checked out the girl and said, "Okay, climb in" as he opened the passenger door for her. Buck walked around to the driver side and got in behind the wheel.

"What is your name?" said Cherry.

"Buck"

"Where are you from?" "Charlotte, NC"

"Well, what are you interested in, Buck from Charlotte, NC?" said Cherry as she reached over and put her hand on Buck's leg. Buck thought the girl was attractive and was interested enough to find out what her price was.

"That kind of depends on how much it would cost me"

Cherry said, "I need a $100 for a blowjob and $150 for both."

"Well, how about this, Cherry? I'll put on a rubber and we fuck for a while and then we take off the rubber and you finish me with a blow job. I'll pay you a buck fifty."

"That sounds good to me," Cherry said as she grabbed Buck's hand and began pulling him back into the sleeper. When they got back in the sleeper, Buck began taking his clothes off. Cherry said, "Whoa, wait a minute cowboy; let's get this money issue out of the way before we get started."

"Okay, said Buck as he reached into his billfold and pulled out a $150 and gave it to Cherry.

"It is not that I don't trust you. It is just that I like to get my money up front. I am sure you can understand, can't you."

"Yea, now let's get naked and have some fun."

Cherry took her clothes of and she looked better naked than she did with her clothes. She had one small tasteful tattoo just above her butt crack. This would be something that Buck could focus on when they were doing it doggie style.

Cherry had a rubber and she opened it and began to put it on Buck's already hard dick. "You have a big one, cowboy, I am not sure I can even get this on you, Cherry said as she struggled to get the rubber stretched to get it over the big head of Buck's dick." Buck helped her and the two of them got it on to their satisfaction.

Buck really did not like to wear a rubber but he did not want to take any chances with someone he did not know.

"How do you want me?" Cherry asked.

It is kinda tight in this sleeper. Why don't you kneel down over the bed and I will put it in from behind. That way I can see your neat tattoo on your back. I like to do it doggie style. How about you?"

"That sounds good to me. Just take it slow at first with that big dick of yours and let me put some lubricant in me. I am still pretty tight."

Buck watched her take a small bottle of lubricant and apply it to her pussy. This really got Buck excited. He was glad she did not shave her pussy. It looked like it had been neatly trimmed around her bikini line and she had some tan lines. Buck admired her perfect, natural, perky breasts. He guessed they were a full C cup or maybe a D. She had a nice tight butt to go with her breasts and really had a good 36-24-36 figure by Buck's speculation.

When Cherry was through rubbing the lubricant in her pussy, she grabbed the pillow from the bed and put it on the floor. She knelt on the pillow and stuck her butt up for Buck to admire. Buck moved behind her and really enjoyed looking at her backside. He could see her pussy trimmed with light brown hair. He could see her tattoo. It was a rose vine with red roses. It was just the right size and decorated Brandy's butt just fine.

Buck had a real steel hard dick and he slowly pushed the head of it into the tight opening of Cherry's pussy. Buck could feel the tightness around the head of his dick. It felt so good that Buck thought he would just put the head in until he thought Brandy was ready for the rest of his shaft. He moved the head of his dick slowly back and forth. Brandy was moaning softly and he got the impression she wanted more when she began really hunching her body back until she had the whole dick in her pussy. Buck was enjoying the sensation of her moving back and forth and he let her do the work. He just kept his body rather still and watched his dick go in and out. It was quite a view and Buck could tell she might get him off without proceeding to the best part. Buck listened to Cherry almost scream out she was coming and he felt her warm liquid discharge. Buck almost came. He exercised some control and slowed down and pulled his dick out of her pussy.

Buck pulled the rubber off and sat down on his bed with his dick sticking up straight and proud. Cherry sat down on the bed beside him and put her mouth on his dick. She knew her way around a man's genitals. She spent a lot of time on the head especially the underside of the head that was so sensitive. Buck thought he would explode and that is just what was about to happen. Cherry tried to deepthroat his long dick but was unable to get quite all of it in her mouth and down her throat. It was deep enough to do the job. Buck warned Cherry was going to come and this seemed inspire her to work harder. She told Buck she wanted him to come all over her face. She could tell he was about to come and she opened her mouth and aimed his dick at it. She jacked it and watched it squirt in her mouth, on her nose, in her eyes and in her hair. Buck really came a lot. He had a three day supply built up and Cherry got it all.

Buck gave her a towel. "Damn cowboy, I never seen anyone with that big a load. You got it up my nose, in my eyes, everywhere," Cherry said as she wiped her face off.

Buck said, "That was great. I would like to see you again. I get through Birmingham a good bit."

"I'll give you a phone number where you can reach me if you know you will be in town." Cherry wrote her number down and gave it to Buck. Buck put her number away. He was really not sure he would call her again or not.

After she was finished dressing, Buck watched her climb out of the truck and walk across the lot to what looked exactly like your typical pimp mobile. The black guy was sitting in it and Buck watched Cherry hand him some money. Then he watched Cherry walk across the lot to a yellow Peterbilt parked beside his truck. The curtain was pulled so Buck could not see who was inside the yellow rig. He watched Cherry climb up in the truck after she had talked to the driver of the yellow truck for a few minutes. Buck tried to see inside the truck but the curtain came all the way around the front windows and he could not see anything inside the truck.

Buck was in his sleeper watching his TV when he heard a scream come from the truck next door. He knew that it was Cherry and she sounded like she was in trouble. Buck got out of his truck and beat on the side of the yellow truck. He could hear a muffled scream from inside. Buck tried to open the door, but it was locked. He went around to the driver side and it was also locked.

Buck beat on the side of the truck and said, "Open up or I am calling the police."

He saw a head peering through the curtain and a gruff looking driver with a full beard said, "You should mind your own business if you know what is good for you." About that time the passenger door of the yellow truck flung open and Cherry almost tumbled out. She looked scared to death. She was running across the parking lot to the pimp mobile. Buck chased after her and they both climbed in the pimp mobile. Cherry said to the black guy sitting in the driver seat, "Leroy, that fucking asshole was going to kill me. He kept trying to get me to drive off with him. I refused and he got me back in his sleeper and I saw an electric chord in his hand. I got scared and screamed. Thank goodness Buck heard me and came and knocked on the side of the truck. It gave me a chance to make a break for it. I grabbed my pocket book and jumped out of the truck. He tried to stop me, but I got away. I am sure he would have killed me. He did not want to pay me anything. I should have known that he was no good."

"Why did you not signal me with your flashlight like you are supposed to do so I could have come out there to see what was the matter?, asked Leroy.

"I was not able to get to my pocketbook. I should have kept it in my hand. He seemed like a nice enough guy until I tried to get him to pay me. I am still shaking, said Cherry."

"You need to be careful, said Leroy. I heard about a girl that got in a truck near Nashville and they found her body down a bank at near a rest area outside of Memphis."

They all looked up to see the yellow truck heading out of the parking lot. Buck could not get a real good look at the driver, but he would recognize the truck if he ever saw it again.

Chapter Six

Charles "Junior" Mitchell grew up in the hills of eastern Tennessee. Many would consider him a "hillbilly". As early as he could remember he went with his father out into the forest where they were cutting logs and loading them on to his dad's truck to deliver them to the paper mill in Canton, NC. He liked going with his father and listening to CB talk on his father's radio. When he was about 14 years old, there was a prostitution ring that would entice truckers to pay them for their services by soliciting them on the CB. Junior would ride with his dad and listen to channel 19 and the girls who talked truckers into stopping at the truck stop at exit 432 on I-40 west. There were several girls that regularly worked the CB. "Dixie Queen", "Daisy Mae", and "Sweet Charlotte" were regulars on channel 19. Junior listened to them and the talk they got from truckers.

Junior was listening to the talk one day. "Daisy Mae" called out, "Hey, any of you truckers out there interested in having some fun today? I am at exit 432 on I-40 west and looking for a good time."

A driver came back, "You sound pretty sexy on this radio. Just what do you mean by wanting to have a good time?"

"Well, you will just have to stop and see. I can't discuss it over the radio if you know what I mean, Good Buddy," came back the reply from Daisy Mae. Junior Mitchell was curious as to what "Daisy Mae" looked like. He heard the trucker come back over the CB, "Well Daisy

Mae, I am coming up on exit 432 and I need a cup of coffee real bad, so I think I will stop. I will be in the green Kenworth with a skateboard hooked to it."

"Okay, big boy, I will be looking for you when you get here," replied Daisy Mae.

Junior did not hear any more transmissions from the pair. He assumed they hooked up when the trucker got to the truck stop. Junior was familiar with the truck stop. He and his Dad had stopped there for breakfast on numerous occasions. There was a big gravel parking lot for trucks and a truckstop with a restaurant and a convenience store. It was not very far from where they were getting loaded with logs.

After the truck got loaded with the logs for the pulp mill, Junior's Dad came back to the truck and they took off for home. They would leave early in the morning for the pulp mill in Canton, NC. They were coming on road where the truck stop was that Daisy Mae met her trucker friend. And Junior asked his Dad if they could stop for a soda. His Dad pulled in the truck stop and they went in the convenience store. Junior's dad was talking with another trucker and Junior saw a girl with real tight blue jean short shorts and a halter top sitting in a black Mustang talking on a CB radio. He could barely make out the conversation since he was close enough to hear the radio.

"Daisy Mae, I am pulling in the truck stop now. I am in the green Kenworth truck,"

crackled the radio.

"I see you driver. I'll come join you when you get parked," came the reply over from the girl in the black mustang.

"I can't get parked quick enough," said the trucker in the green Kenworth truck.

Junior saw the green Kenworth truck back in an empty parking space and he saw the girl get out of the mustang. Junior watched the girl go down to the truck and talk to the driver. He could not hear the conversation. But he saw her walk around to the passenger side of the truck and climb up in it. Junior was excited thinking about what would take place inside the truck and he reached down to adjust his hard dick in his pants. It was sticking out like a tent pole.

"What are you looking at, boy. You better stay away from women like that. They will ruin you." I knew a trucker that spent all his money on a whore like that and he got the claps to boot. You are not old enough now, but you listen to what I say. Stay away from women like that and you will be a lot better off," Junior's father said to Junior.

If your Mother saw you even looking at her like that, she would swear you were lusting after her and you would go straight to hell," he continued.

"Dad, I heard her on the CB. She is Daisy Mae. She talks to truckers over the CB. I heard her talking to that driver in the green Kenworth truck and I saw her go get in it with him," said Junior.

WHACK, Junior's dad smacked Junior on the back of his head. "I told you, son, not to even think about women like that. It is a sin to lust after women and especially a whore like that. Come on. Let's go. I am going to tell your mother about this when we get home."

Junior got a thorough scolding from his mother when he got home. She was sure he was going to hell for his lust in his loins. Junior's mother was a born again southern baptist and she had preached to him many times about not having unclean thoughts in his head. He had heard this many times before and he would hear it many more times before he got out of the house. He could not wait to get old enough to get out of the house and be on his own.

Junior drove the logging truck for his dad for a few years when he was old enough to get CDL. He drove for 6 months with his Dad on a permit. Then he got his CDL when he was old enough. His dad got sick when Junior was 18 and junior had to do all the driving. He really did not want to drive a logging truck back and forth from Chestnut Hill, Tennessee to Canton, NC. He wanted to drive over the road. When his dad died a year later, Junior inherited his father's truck. He had saved enough money to get a better truck. He got a yellow Peterbilt that was a few years old. It was in good shape and Junior began pulling a flatbed all over the country. He got his loads from a freight broker in Knoxville, Tennessee.

Junior learned which truck stops had "lot lizards" and he liked fooling around with them. One night in Indianapolis things took a turn for the bad. Junior was in his sleeper and heard a knock on his door. He looked out the window and saw a young girl about 20 years old standing beside his truck. "Would you like some company, Driver?" The young girl said.

"Sure," replied Junior.

The young girl walked around to the passenger side of the truck and climbed in the cab. She sat down in the passenger seat and said with a big smile, "My name is Brandy, what is yours?" Junior replied that his name was Jack. They were both lying but it was a start to the real conversation. "How much money you got, Jack? Do you want to spend some with me for me to give you some real pleasure? You have been on the road all day and I can take good care of you if you want to pay me for my time."

"That depends," said Junior, "on what you have in mind and how much it will cost." "I'll give you and blowjob and a fuck for $150. If you want something less, we can negotiate it out, said Brandy.

"I'll pay you a $150 if you can get me off," said Junior.

"Oh, I can get you off unless you have some problem and can't get off," replied Brandy.

"Don't worry about me. I can get off. I'll pay you when you get me off."

"Oh no, I don't work that way. I have to be paid up front. Come on Jack, I know you will enjoy it."

Junior reluctantly reached into his billfold and pulled out $150 cash and gave it to Brandy. Brandy took the money and folded it into her pocketbook. She reached over and started rubbing Jack's dick. They crawled back into the sleeper of the truck and began taking their clothes off. Brandy got his dick hard and started putting a rubber on it. It would not stay hard and she kept alternating between sucking his dick and trying to get the rubber on and it became futile. Junior went along with this for a while and then he told Brandy that he would have to fuck her without a rubber if he was going to get off. Brandy would not agree to that. Junior began to get impatient and frustrated with her.

He finally got it hard enough to get the rubber on and then he told Brandy to bend over doggie style. He started fucking her and kept it up for about 15 minutes.

Brandy said "We are going to have to stop. I don't think you are going to finish and we are out of time."

"Out of time, Bitch! I'll show you out of time, shouted Junior. And he reached over and grabbed wooden nightstick he kept under his seat and whacked Brandy over the head. Just to make sure she was dead he took a rubber tie down strap and wrapped it around her neck and tied it in a tight knot to shut off her airway. The he laid her out and finished what he had started with her. He actually seemed to get more excited with her being completely immobile.

After Junior was sure she was completely lifeless, he got out of the truck to see if anybody was watching his truck. It was dark and quiet around his truck, so he got back in and drove off. It was close to midnight by this time and there was not much traffic on the road. After he had driven about an hour and a half out of Indianapolis, he pulled of the side of the road where there was a steep embankment. He made sure there was not any traffic. And he put the dead girl's body in a trash bag and threw it out of the truck down the steep embankment. Junior got back into his truck and drove off into the night.

Chapter Seven

Buck pulled in to Uncle Willie's Truck Stop outside of Nashville. It had good home cooking and he was hungry. He sat down at the bar beside another trucker. After a few minutes the trucker turned to Buck and said, "They had some excitement this morning here. The police were here. They discovered a naked girl in a trash bag in the dumpster. She had been reported missing for a few days. Apparently she was a lot lizard from somewhere else." "For real?" Buck asked.

"Yea, no shit. She was a young girl about 20 years old. Found her without a stitch on. Apparently she was strangled with a rubber load strap. It was still wrapped around her neck."

"Yea, no shit"

"Hey, have you ever seen a yellow Peterbilt stay here?"

"Can't say as I have. I don't spend the night here a lot. I eat here a good bit. I like the food."

"Yea, me too. The reason I asked was that I saw a yellow Peterbilt truck down in Birmingham and the driver tried to get rough with a hooker there and she got away with her life. I did not get a good look at the driver. I would know the truck if I saw it again."

"I have heard a driver talking on the CB the other day and there have been a number of lot lizards which have disappeared at truck stops all the way from Illinois to Florida."

"That can't be too good for the hooker business, can it?" said Buck.

"No, I would not think so," said the other Driver.

Buck had a load going to Laredo, Texas, so he could not stay around and chat very long. He said goodbye to the driver and finished his meal and went to pay for his meal. Buck asked the checkout girl if the girl the police pulled out of the dumpster was a local girl. The checkout girl said she nobody here recognized her.

The girl went on to say, "The police think she was murdered somewhere else and the murderer dumped her body here in our dempster dumpster. The police were asking about a yellow Peterbilt rig in here with Tennessee license plates. So they must have some idea the murderer was a trucker. That is scary isn't it?"

"It sure is and I think I know the truck they are looking for. I think I had a bit of a run-in with the same truck in Birmingham not too long ago. I will know that truck if I see it again."

Buck left Nashville on his way to Laredo, Texas wondering if he would ever see the yellow Peterbilt truck again what he might do if he saw it. It was a good 2 day trip to Laredo and Buck drove about ten and a half hours before he took his ten hour break. He spent the night in Texarkana, Texas. With no bad luck, he could make it in to Laredo by tomorrow night. Buck made it into Laredo the next night, which was a Friday night and dropped his trailer on the drop yard. Since it was a weekend, he did not think he would be getting a load out of Laredo until Monday morning and it was time for his truck to be serviced; he put his truck in the shop at the terminal.

On Saturday Buck was resting in the drivers lounge at the terminal watching the TV and he got into a conversation with one of the drivers. The driver asked Buck if he had ever gone to Nuevo Laredo. Laredo was a border town and Nuevo Laredo was on the other side of the Mexican border. The driver told Buck that he ought to go over there to a place called *Boy's Town*. He told him that *Boy's Town* was a place that was full of bars and good looking Mexican prostitutes. He said you can take your pick and negotiate with them and could get a piece of ass for about thirty or forty dollars. The girls did not speak much English, but they understood enough to let you fuck them. The driver told Buck he had gone last night and he was going back tonight. He did not get to see the donkey show. He told me that around 9 o'clock every night they had a donkey show and a woman came out with a donkey and let the donkey fuck her. Buck could not believe it. Buck told the driver that he wanted to go with him.

The driver's name was Jimmy. Jimmy said, "OK, if you want to go, we need to be at the Pilot Truck stop down the road, and catch a ride with a guy called Cowboy at 5 o'clock. Let me call him and make sure he is not filled up already. Jimmy called and asked Cowboy if he had room for two more. Buck heard Jimmy ask him if he could pick us up at the Whiteline terminal. When Jimmy hung up with Cowboy, he told Buck that we were in and Cowboy would just pick us up here at our terminal around 4:45. So I'll meet you here about 4:30 this afternoon. OK?"

Buck said "Yea, thanks"

Jimmy went on to say, "Cowboy drives a passenger van and he charges twenty-five dollars to carry you across the border and back. He knows how to get through the border patrol, so it is well worth it. A taxi would charge you twice as much for one way." Jimmy said, "I would not take any extra money and I would hide what I did take. I never take my billfold and I don't take over 400 to 500 dollars. Everything is so cheap over there; I cannot imagine spending more than about 300 dollars. I have never had any trouble, but you see a lot of people that look like they would like to get their hands on some money, and you hear stories of people getting robbed across the border in Mexico."

So Cowboy showed up right on schedule and Buck and Jimmy were waiting on him. They climbed in the van and headed for the border.

Cowboy stopped at several truckstops along the way and picked up about a dozen truckers. He carried them through the border patrol and on into Nuevo Laredo, Mexico. When they got to *Boys Town*, he let them out and said he would be leaving at 11:00 o'clock sharp. Buck and Jimmy went to a place called Pappagallos and sat down and had a drink. Buck was not drinking any alcohol. He wanted a clear head if he was going to be with any women while he was there. They had not been sitting in the bar very long when an attractive but older Mexican woman came over to their table.

She said, "Where are you boys from?"

Jimmy said he was from Phoenix and Buck told her he was from Charlotte, North Carolina.

She went on to say her name was Rosallita and she asked them what their names were. They told her their names. She sat down beside Buck and put her hand o his leg. She did not stop with his thigh, but continued to slide her hand up into his crotch. She said "You boys just let me know if you are interested in anything besides a drink. She gave Buck's dick a little squeeze and she smiled at him when she realized how big his dick was. It began getting a hard on as soon as she touched his leg. Buck had shorts on and his dick was at the end of his pants. Rosallita stroked his dick and then she reached under his pants leg and squeezed the head of his dick. Rosallita said she would show him a real good time for 50 dollars. Then she grabbed his hand and tried to get Buck to follow her. Buck thought for a minute and said. "I think I will wait a while and maybe take you up on that a little later." Rosallita said, "OK, I will be here all day." She move on to another table and Buck tried to relax. He had gotten pretty turned on and he was surprised that he could put Rosalitta off like he did. Jimmy said, "I think she really wanted you. Why did you not go with her."

Buck said, "I want to see what else is here before I go off with the first girl I see. I would kinda like to see if I can find a good looking girl that is maybe a little younger than her."

About that time a guy came over to their table. He asked if we drove for Whiteline. I guess he saw it written on or caps. He said he used to drive for Whiteline. They had let him go after he had an accident near Fayetteville, North Carolina. He did not say it but I think their might have also been a problem with him passing the drug screen after the accident. That is something that Whiteline would not tolerate. His name was Bill, but everybody called him "Slim." Slim found out it was my first time at *Boys Town* and he said he could show us around and he could speak Spanish and help us communicate while we were here. He went on to say that we did not want to miss the "Donkey Show" at 9 o'clock at the bar at the end of the street. He explained that this girl fucked a donkey. He was very descriptive. He said she would grab that big ole donkey dick and shove it up her pussy. He said that donkey would squirt everywhere.

Slim said, "Come on, I want to show you the best girls here." So we walked around the block to where there were rows of little one story apartments. In front of most of the apartments would be a scantily dressed girl sitting in a chair smiling at us. Some of them would say "fucky, sucky" or something similar to get our attention. Slim said most of these girls did not speak much English. He took us down to an apartment at the end of the short street and knocked on the door. A good looking young Hispanic girl opened the door. He said something to her in Spanish and she looked at us. The girl was wearing what looked like something out of the Arabian Nights. It was a "see through" flimsy top and pants. Under it the girl had on bikini panties and bra. She could not have been more than 20 years old. Buck was ready. He told Slim to ask her what it would cost to fuck with her on top and then turn over and do doggie style and then take off the rubber and she would finish him with a blow job and hand job. Buck knew what he wanted. Slim and the girl talked in Spanish again. Slim told Buck it would be 30 dollars unless he took longer than 15 minutes. It would be 20 more dollars if he took longer than 15 minutes. Buck said he would probably not take more than 15 minutes.

He explained sometimes it took him longer when he used a rubber. Buck said tell her that and she if she will do it for 30 dollars. Slim talked to the girl and then turned to Buck and said she agreed to do it for 30 dollars.

The girl took Buck's hand and closed the door behind him. She led him over to the bed and took out a rubber from the drawer in the bedside table. She pointed to Buck and motioned for him to get undressed. Buck asked her if she spoke any English. She said she spoke "a little bit."

"What is your name?" asked Buck. "My name is Carmen, "she replied.

Carmen took all her clothes off and she had a magnificent body. She had a small waist and firm round titties with big dark aureoles. She had a triangular shaped natural bush of dark hair which matched her long flowing shiny flowing hair on top of her head. She must have put on some lotion. Her skin looked soft and smooth and she smelled like orchids in full bloom. Buck liked everything about her. She put her hand on his dick and gave it a gentle squeeze. Buck was about half hard when she did this and it really got his dick to stand up long and proud.

Carmen looked up to Buck and said "grande." After she got the rubber on Buck's massive boner, which was no easy task, she laid down on the full sized bed and spread her legs.

Buck looked at her and said, "You are bonito." She smiled and Buck knew that she understood what he was saying to her. Buck started to mount the lovely girl and she held up her hand and said "esperar." She reached over into the night stand and got some lubricant and she put some on Buck's dick and rubbed a little on her pussy lips. Buck then eased up to her with his dick in his hand and put the head of his dick up against her tight opening. He went slow and he could feel she was real tight. He moved in and out real slow and was only putting about half of the length of his dick inside her. He could tell that she was not in any discomfort by her facial expressions. She began to really enjoy it and she placed both hands on his butt and tried to pull him in deeper. Buck was going faster and deeper and he knew that as tight as she was, he was not going to last long at this rate. It was feeling too good.

He said to Carmen, "Let's turn over," as he motioned with his hands. She flipped over and stuck her beautiful smooth butt up in the air for him to admire and penetrate with his massive hard dick. Buck had to stop and just look at the sight for a moment. Her skin was so smooth and she had the most exquisite butt Buck has ever seen. It was almost but not quite what you would call a bubblebutt. But the sight of her small puckered dark asshole and the vertical smile below it with the tufts of hair surrounding it was almost too much for Buck. He thought he would explode and fill the rubber with cum before he got to slide his dick inside her pussy lips down into the warm, wet vaginal canal. She had nice pussy lips, not too big and not too small. From the rear you could watch them seem to hug his dick as he pulled his dick back for the downstroke. Buck tried to think of something to keep from cumming. He wanted to get to the last part of the session before he came and it was a struggle. He could tell he was ready to come. She had a way of squeezing his dick as he withdrew it and it was really getting him to the exploding point. He started adding numbers in his head, trying to sing songs, anything to keep from cumming. She was really fucking him now – hard and fast, and deep. He knew he had to stop and he knew he was well short of the 15 minute session he was shooting for.

He pulled his dick out and laid on his back and pulled the rubber off. His dick was sticking straight up and it looked bigger than ever. The head of the dick looked like a big purple mushroom. Carmen looked at it and smiled. She laid across his body and grabbed hold of is dick. She put her mouth on the head of his dick and jacked the shaft gently with her hand. She licked his dick like it was a lollipop. Buck could only see the back of her head and her long flowing black hair. The sensations were too much. He laid his head back and closed his eyes and let the excitement mount. Buck did not know how she did it. No one had ever done it before, but she was able somehow to get the entire length of his dick down her throat. Carmen would alternate licking the head of his dick while stroking his dick with her hand, and then sliding the dick all the way down her throat. Buck could not take very muck of this. He announced to Carmen, "I am going to cum."

Carmen took her mouth off his dick and squeezed it with her hand. She stroked it very slowly up and down. It began to squirt. She had his dick pointed straight up and watched it squirt. It was like a volcano erupting. The first squirt was small and did not got very high the next squirt was every bit of 5 feet into the air and landed on his stomach. There were successive blasts each squirting high in the air for 6-8 more times. Carmen had pretty good aim because all the cum, which was a lot, landed on Buck's stomach. When it was through squirting, Carmen gave it one last squeeze and got the last drop of cum out. Buck felt relaxed and completely drained. Carmen got up as he laid on the bed in the afterglow that only comes after a great session of sex. Carmen brought him a warm rag and wiped off his stomach.

"Do you feel better now?" Carmen asked. Buck said "I feel wonderful.

Buck gave Carmen an extra 10 dollars and still could not believe he had gotten such a great fuck and suck for 40 dollars. He caught back up with Slim at Pappagallos, which was where they had agreed to meet. Slim said Jimmy had gone off with another girl. Slim asked how he liked Carmen and Buck said she was great and he gave her an extra 10 dollars. She was well worth it.

Slim told Buck that they could stay here or check out the rest of the place. *Boys Town* was not very big. It was about two city blocks with nothing but bars and apartments with girls sitting outside of each apartment. It was every man's dream and Buck wanted to check out the rest of it. So they left Papagallos and went up the street. Slim was a great guide. He told him that the girls working inside the bars generally charged more than the ones outside their apartments. He said the ones in the bars had to give the bar a take because the bar generally furnished them a room. They went in a couple of bars and Buck bought Slim a few beers. It was so cheap, he could not believe it. Buck was still only drinking water or ginger ale. Buck was getting hungry so he got a couple of tacos from a street vendor. They tasted very good or else he was very hungry.

Every bar they went into, girls would come up to them and sit down with them. Slim would talk to them in Spanish and translate for Buck. None of the girls were bashful. They would put their hands on your dick and ask you if you wanted some pussy. Buck especially liked one of the girls. She said she wanted to get on his truck and come with him to the States. Buck said that would be great. She could teach him Spanish and he could teach her English. After several of these bar girls played with Buck's dick through his pants, he was ready for action again. He and Slim went out and walked past the apartments with the girls out front. Buck stopped and talked with one of the girls sitting in front of her apartment. She was a real attractive Hispanic girl about 20 years old. She could not speak much English so Slim translated for Buck and he negotiated a price that both Buck and the girl were in agreement.

The girl said her name was Marie. She was very efficient. As soon as Buck got in her apartment she unzipped his pants and pulled out his long dick. She looked at it and smiled at Buck. She unwrapped a rubber from its package and worked it on to Buck's dick. She took off her panties and stretched out straddle-legged on the bed. Buck paused for a moment to admire her beautiful body. She had perky breasts with big round dark aureoles. She had an absolutely pretty pussy with a narrow landing strip of hair above the top of her pussy. She was meticulously shaved outside of this landing strip of dark pubic hair. He could see her pussy lips sticking out of her opening. He could tell the lips were a darker color of brown and were already wet. He could see a wet creamy liquid on the lips of her pussy. She had her legs spread but the slit of her pussy was not gapped open.

It was a beautiful sight. She looked very inviting and she had a beautiful smile. Buck could not wait any longer. He was ready and he mounted her. She was tight and it was difficult to get his dick inside her. He went slow and eased his dick all the way inside up the base of his shaft. Marie kept smiling as he penetrated the depths of her vagina. She reached back and grabbed his buttocks and pulled him into her all the way. She was very tight but she could handle the entire length of his penis without any discomfort. She kept smiling and kept pulling him up against her as Buck began to hump her faster. She had her legs up in the air spread wide apart and she began to moan as Buck kept up the pace. She evidently liked it hard and fast. Buck could feel his climax beginning to build. He wanted to make it last. He told her to turn over and do it doggie style. She looked at him and he could tell she did not understand. Buck made a motion with his two hands imitating a turning over motion. She understood this and told Buck that new position would be 20 more dollars. Buck nodded in agreement.

Marie turned over and got on her knees. Buck really liked the view from the rear. Marie had her butt stuck up in the air and he could see her slit between her thighs. It was clean shaven with no stubble and her butthole was really very nice. It was dark in color and a perfect circle with evenly spaced wrinkles surrounding the tight opening. Buck got more excited as he admired her backside. He butt was absolutely perfect- smooth and round with no blemishes at all.

Marie wiggled her butt from side to side and Buck eased up to her inviting opening. He grabbed his dick and guided it into the tight pussy. Marie moaned as he slid his dick inside her. Buck fucked her hard and fast. She loved it. He put his finger up against her butthole as he fucked her. He could tell she did not mind this and she was getting more excited. He slipped his finger inside her butt and she began to moan louder and move her but backup against it. Buck had his finger inside her butt and was fucking her hard and fast. He pulled his dick out and pushed it up against her butthole. Marie pulled away and looked back at Buck. She said, "Fuck my butt is 20 more dollars." Buck thought a minute and shook his head in agreement.

Marie stuck her butt back up in the air and wiggled it at Buck. Buck made sure the rubber was still on securely and he inserted his dick into Marie's pretty butthole. It was tight at first and very hard to get it in. Buck kept pushing it in and Marie kept pushing back on his rock hard pole. He pumped it in and out and after several attempts he got it almost all the way in. He could tell this was a s far as it was going to go, so he began pumping it in and out. Marie was squealing like a pig by this time and Buck did not hold back. He fucked her tight little ass hard and fast. Marie squealed and he could tell she was about to climax. Buck could tell she was not faking. She was really enjoying it. Buck slapped her ass and she squealed louder. He slapped her ass with both hands and she reached her climax. Buck could tell by the way she screamed out.

Buck was about to cum. He stopped and turned over and laid on the bed. He motioned for Marie to get on top. Marie said, "New position, 20 more dollars." By this time Buck did not care. He nodded his head and said, "Ok, get me off, I can't stop now" He did not think she understood anything except she would get 20 more dollars. Marie stopped long enough to put a new rubber on Buck and then she mounted him. She was good in this position. She knew just how to pump him up and down and then sit all the way down on his dick and grind back and forth on it. Buck did not last long, as he came, he grabbed with both hands on her flanks. He held still as he pumped one jet of sperm after another into the rubber. After he was through, he pulled his dick out and laid on the bed in total satisfaction and relaxation. Marie pulled the rubber off is dick and threw it away. She gave him a warm rag to wash himself off. Buck said "gracius, senorita," as he reached into his pants and gave her 60 more dollars. Buck did not feel cheated in the least. It was a business proposition and he could not think of a better use of 60 dollars. Marie took the money and said, "gracias."

Buck left her apartment and looked at his watch. It was almost time for the donkey show. Buck was headed for the Yellow Cactus Bar, where the donkey show was to take place. He turned the corner into one of the side streets of the little village of apartments and two Mexicans came up to him. There was not much room to pass on the narrow street and the next thing Buck saw was that one of the Mexicans had a gun in his hand. Buck looked up at the guy with the gun and heard him say, "Stop, Gringo, and give me your money!"

Buck responded, "Not so fast, Hombre, Are you going to shoot me with that thing?" as he pointed to his pistol. When the Mexican looked down, Buck moved as fast as lightning and knocked the gun out of the Mexican's hand with his left hand and came across with his right hand and smacked the Mexican full on the side of his head. The blow was so fast and hard the Mexican spun around and fell to the ground. Buck saw the other Mexican coming at him out of the corner of his eye and he gave him a swift kick to the midsection. This made the second Mexican double over and he fell to the ground. Buck quickly picked up the pistol and said, "Get your ass out of my sight, before I decide to use this gun on you." The Mexicans knew enough English to know that they did not need to mess with Buck anymore. The quickly got to their feet and ran off around the corner. Buck stuck the gun in his pocket and went on to the donkey show.

There was a crowd gathering inside the bar as Buck got there. He was able to get a front row seat next to the stage so he sat down and waited on the show to begin. He had seen the donkey outside the bar in his corral on the way into the bar. In a few minutes, the handler brought the donkey into the bar and tied him to a pole. The donkey apparently was already excited. His long, pink dick was sticking out of its sheath about 3-4 feet in anticipation of what was about to happen.

In a few minutes a girl in a frilly squirt came out onto the stage with the donkey. There was some Latin music playing in the background and the girl danced around the stage in front of the donkey for a few minutes. The donkey was watching the girl and seemed to be enjoying the show. You could tell his dick got even longer. It was sticking out from under its back legs a good four feet up to its front legs and almost touching the ground. The girl had stopped dancing and had walked up beside the donkey she was talking to it and rubbing it and she kissed him on the nose. She bent over and the frilly dress came up and you could see she had on a red thong. She had a real nice ass which the audience had a good view of as she danced around the donkey. After rubbing the donkey for a few minutes, the girl reached down and grabbed the long pink shaft under the donkey. She grabbed it about 6-8 inches from its end and bent over. She took one hand and slid her thong over out of the way and thrust the long shaft into her pussy. It was difficult to tell how far inside she got the long donkey into her. But you could watch her hand go in and out. It did not take the donkey long. He made a braying noise and the girl pulled the shaft out and you could see donkey cum squirting out of the donkey's dick. Buck watched several squirts and one of them almost hit him. It landed on the stage in front of him. The donkey must have squirted a pint of spunk out and it landed all over the stage. The stage was only about 15 feet X 15 feet and Buck noticed that there were a lot of stains on the floor from previous performances. Buck realized this donkey got plenty of action. The girl bowed to the audience and had the donkey bow to the audience, and then they both left the stage to a large round of applause.

Buck looked at is watch and realized that he had about an hour and a half before he was to meet Cowboy for the trip back. He went back over to Pappagallos. Slim was sitting at a table with a good looking Latino girl. Buck went over and sat down next to her. Buck told Slim he was having a wonderful day at *Boys Town*. Buck told Slim about his adventures of the day including the attempted robbery. And he gave Slim the gun. He could get into trouble with Whiteline if he had a gun on his truck. It was against company policy and was illegal in a lot of states Buck travelled through to have a concealed weapon on his truck.

The Latino girl eased over beside Buck and asked him to buy her a drink. Buck told her to order what she wanted. She told Buck her name was Victoria and she slid her hand along Buck's leg until she was holding his dick through his pants. Buck's dick immediately began to elongate. He was wearing shorts and it extended almost to the end of his shorts. Victoria realized this and she reached under the pants leg and wrapped her fingers around the head of his dick. She looked up at Buck with a smile and asked him if he wanted to go to her room. Buck asked her what it would cost him and she said $50 for a date with her. Buck said "I have already been with two other girls and I am not sure I can go again."

Victoria said, "I am sure you can go again and she gave his dick a squeeze." Buck was getting real excited. By this time she was stroking his dick up and down. Victoria was a very good looking girl. She had long dark hair that shimmered in the lights. Her eyes were green and had a sparkle when she smiled. Her body looked perfect. She was very shapely and you could tell she was just naturally well built and good looking. She had not had any cosmetic surgery anywhere on her body and there were no visible tattoos or piercings. Buck did not care for tattoos or body piercings. Buck guessed she was about his age – 26 or so. Buck looked at his watch and decided he had enough time to go to her room and still catch his ride back to the truck stop. Buck was afraid if she kept up what she was doing, he would explode in his pants. Buck said, "OK, Victoria, let's go."

Victoria went behind the bar and got a key to a room. Evidently the rooms were furnished by the owner of the bar. She led Buck through a door down a long hall of rooms to one about halfway down the hall. She put the key in the door and opened it. She grabbed Buck's hand and led him into the room. The room was very nice compared to the small one bedroom apartments outside the in the village. It had a big king size bed with an expensive looking comforter and pillow cases. Victoria told Buck to give her $50 and go get undressed and take a shower she would join him in a minute.

Buck complied with her requests. He was in the shower and Victoria came in and got in the shower with him. She was magnificent. She had full round breasts and a nice, shapely butt. She let him touch her breasts and rub his stiff dick against her body. She was interested in making sure his dick was clean. Buck figured since he had been with some other women, she wanted to make sure he would not give her anything she did not want. She was very delicate in the way she rubbed soap all over his dick and balls. She really knew how to stroke a dick with her hands. He already knew this from the bar, but the sensations were increased with a soapy lather in the shower. She stroked him up and down and he thought he might explode in the shower. He pulled away slightly and then got around behind her and rubbed his dick up and down on the crack of her ass while he reached around and fondled her boobs with his hands. She seemed to enjoy this and she pressed her butt back against his long, hard manhood. Buck rubbed her nipples with his fingers and he could feel them stiffen up in his grasp.

Buck slid his dick in between her legs and she spread her legs and guided the head of his dick into her warm, wet pussy. Buck was going crazy with desire. Her pussy felt wonderful. He had never felt anything so good. He held onto her and pumped his dick in and out of her. Victoria sighed and said, "Let's go get in bed, Baby." Buck stopped and got out of the shower and dried off as fast as he could. He stretched out naked on the bed and waited for Victoria. She came over to him and leaned over and put her mouth on his long dick. She ran her tongue all over the purple head of his dick. She grasped the shaft ever so gently and slid her mouth and hand up and down on it at the same time. Buck could hardly stand it without blowing his load all over the bed. He pulled her head away from his dick after a few minutes of this exquisite pleasure. He told her to get on her knees and he got behind her. Doggie style was his favorite position and Victoria seemed to like it as well. She got on her knees and stuck her beautiful butt up in the air for Buck to admire. Buck thought to himself that she was beautiful from this vantage point as he was putting his rubber on. He could see her clean shaven, puffy crotch. She had long dark, wet pussy lips hanging down from her pussy. He could not wait to get his dick back inside her. Her pussy was tight and she could squeeze the head of his dick as he withdrew it. Buck had not been sure he could go a third time before he started, but he was sure of it now. He could feel his balls tighten and knew his load was going to come squirting out. Buck pumped harder and knew he could not hold out much longer. He stopped and laid back down on the bed. He took his rubber off and told Victoria to finish him off. She seemed delighted to perform this request. She grabbed his dick and stroked it. Then she would stop and put her lips on his dick and suck for a while. She could tell when he was about to cum and she would stop. She alternated giving him head and jacking his dick for several minutes and each time he would get close, she would stop. Buck was going out of his mind with pleasure and he watched Victoria as she kept her program up. She seemed to be enjoying watching him go crazy. Buck was pleading with her now, "Don't stop," he would say. But each time he got close, she would stop. "Please, I want to cum," Buck would say. Victoria would say not yet, baby," and she would start pumping up and down with her hand and then she would put her mouth on his shaft and slide it up and down. Buck could not take it anymore. Victoria knew he was about to cum and she stopped and just watched his dick as it throbbed back and forth and then it erupted. Cum came out the top of his dick and squirted on his stomach. Buck felt a tremendous relief as load was spent.

Victoria did a surprising thing after he finished shooting his load. She took her finger and mopped up some of the cum with it and put it in her mouth. "Uuuummm," she said, "your cum tastes good, Buck. "I need to eat some protein every day. I sure do like your brand." Victoria went onto say, "I want to go to the USA. Take me with you on your truck, OK? I have a brother in Nashville" Buck knew what they just experienced with each other was more than your usual business transaction, and he appreciated it, but he really was not expecting her to want to go with him on his truck. He thought about this and was trying to figure out a way to make it happen.

Buck told Victoria it was against company policy to carry a rider with you because of insurance reasons. The rider was not covered if anything happened. He told her they would have to be very careful and it is against the law. They could get into serious trouble if the border patrol caught him. Buck said he knew about a driver that carried some Mexicans across the border without even knowing it. They were hid in the shroud above the cab of the tractor and they rode with him across the border until he stopped. The driver heard them talking on a cell phone when he stopped, and then he saw them jump down and run when he stopped at a rest area for a pee break. There were three Mexicans riding on top of his truck and they all jumped down and ran when he stopped. Vitoria said, "I could do that and if they caught me at border patrol, I would tell them, you did not know I was up there. Buck got dressed and they talked about their plans and Victoria agreed to have sex with him without charging him for as long as she was on his truck. Buck certainly liked that part of the arrangement.

Buck said, "I go through Nashville a lot and there is a good chance I will be going through there in the next couple of days." He told her he would call her when he knew where his next load would take him when he got back to the terminal. Victoria said she could meet at the truck stop near the terminal, which was already across the border in the USA. She knew a way to get there without being caught. She could hide in the top of his truck until they passed the border patrol check station just out of town. Buck had never been stopped by the border patrol before. Whiteline trucks were not scrutinized very closely because they had a reputation for doing everything by the book. He did not anticipate any problems if she could get to the truck stop. Buck cautioned her about talking to anyone about his involvement. Victoria agreed not to say anything to anybody until they were in the states.

Buck got back to the Pappagallos, which was the meeting place, and he rode with Cowboy back to his terminal.

Chapter Eight

Buck got back to his terminal and found out his truck was ready to roll. He checked with the dispatch and found out he had load going to Nashville, Tennessee. He called Victoria and told her he would be leaving in about an hour for Nashville. Victoria told Buck she would get a ride to the truck stop and would be waiting on him. It was about midnight, so they would be hitting the border patrol about 0130. Buck took a quick shower and changed into his work clothes. He got his Bill of Lading from the dispatch window at the terminal. After he got his truck keys from the shop, he found his trailer on the yard by its number. He backed his tractor up under it and heard the fifth wheel lock around the trailer kingpin. He got out and hooked the electrical hose and the air lines to the trailer. He made a quick inspection of the trailer and his truck. When he was satisfied with everything, he pulled up to the fuel pumps and filled both tanks with fuel. Then he pulled onto the scales at the terminal and made sure his weight was legal. Buck put his loaded call into the Quallcomm and waited to be dispatched. The computer would double check everything and make sure the load was correct and the right trailer was going to the right place. In just a minute, the computer beeped and the message said he was dispatched to the Whiteline terminal in Nashville.

Buck pulled up to the terminal gate and, which was the final checkpoint before he left. The voice came over the intercom, "Truck number?" Buck replied, "Truck number 31532." "You are good to go, driver, have a safe trip." The gate opened and Bucked pulled out of the yard. He was finally on his way to Nashville. He called Victoria again and she said she was on her way to the truck stop and would be there in 10 minutes. Buck said that was great. He told her to meet him in the vacant lot across the street from the truck stop. It would be a better place for her to climb up on top of the tractor. They had to pass one checkpoint at the border control station about 5 miles up the interstate. All trucks had to pull into the checkpoint. Buck had never had his truck pulled over for an inspection of his cab at this checkpoint, nor had he ever seen any other Whiteline truck pulled over for an inspection.

Buck pulled into the vacant lot across from the truckstop and waited for Victoria. She arrived in an old chevy in a few minutes and said she had got across the border with no problems. She hid in a hidden compartment that was big enough for one person located under the back seat. Buck took her bag and put it in the compartment under the sleeper.

"I am glad you made it, Victoria. We are going to have a good time on the truck after we get past the checkpoint. Are we ready to go?" Buck asked. Victoria answered, "Si, Buck. We go to USA"

Buck helped her get up on top of the cab of the truck and under the wind shroud. He gave her a blanket to cover up with and he said, " The check point is about five miles up the road. Make sure you are lying down under the blanket when we get there. Remember, if you get caught, you are on your own. I will tell them I did not know you were up there."

Buck walked around the truck to make sure you could not tell she was hiding on his roof and then he got in his truck and cranked it up. He took off up the interstate, driving just like he would have if he did not have a passenger on his roof. Buck got to the checkpoint and waited in line for two trucks ahead of him. He could see the border patrol had about 3 guys outside talking and they had a drug sniffing dog with them. That made Buck a little uneasy. The two trucks in front of him were waved on without a problem and when he got to the guardhouse, the man in the guardhouse asked what was he carrying, which was customary. Buck responded, "retail merchandise." It was a load of dry goods that would eventually end up in Wal-Mart. Buck stared at the red light for a few seconds and saw it turn green and heard the guard say "go ahead." Buck felt a big relief and proceeded ahead. The guards on the other side were still talking and if they had even looked up at his truck, he did not know it. Buck drove up the road probably 8-10 miles and pulled off at an off ramp. He helped Victoria down from the top of his truck and told her to get in the cab.

"We made it. It would be better if you stayed in the sleeper for a while," said Buck. "I am not supposed to have a rider. Like I told you, it has something to do with our insurance. We will stop up the road and get something to eat. I have got to make it as far as Texarkana to stay on schedule."

"Okay," said Victoria and she climbed into the sleeper.

Buck had been driving several hours and was making good time up the interstate when Victoria crawled out of the sleeper. She was on her hands and knees and slid up beside the driver's seat. Buck had on a pair of loose shorts and Victoria slid her hand up inside them and squeezed Buck's dick. Buck instantly got a raging hard on when he felt Victoria's hand on his dick. She pulled his long shaft out from his shorts and began stroking it. Buck slid over in the seat to give her better access to his manhood. He had the truck on cruise control and there was very little traffic so he sat back and let Victoria continue to caress his long dick. She was stroking it and she put her lips around the head of his shaft. Buck was getting more excited by the second. Victoria put her hand around his balls and tried to deepthroat his long shaft. She was not able to get the entire length into her mouth even though she tried very hard. It felt real good to Buck anyway having most of his dick inside her warm mouth and throat.

Victoria kept the stroking and sucking up for several minutes and Buck knew he would not be able to hold off much longer. He was real excited by this time and he thought it might be a good idea to pull off the highway. Fortunately there was a rest area coming up and Buck pulled into it. He found a vacant truck parking space away from all the other trucks and he quickly pulled the rig into it and shut it off. He got up from the seat and took his shorts off and sat down in the sleeper. Victoria pulled her top off and and guided his hard dick in between her tits. She fucked him with her tits for a few minutes.

Buck decided he wanted to put his dick inside Victoria's pussy. He pulled her shorts off and lay her down beside him on the sleeper. They were in the spoon position. Buck reached both hands around her body and massaged her tits. He was thrusting his still hard dick in between her legs. He could feel her moist opening and he felt her reach down with her hand and guide his dick into the opening of her wet pussy. From this position Buck was able to get about half the length of his shaft into her opening. Buck slid down a little and was able to get the entire length into her hole. It felt wonderful and Buck was thrusting real hard by this time. He felt his juices begin to build pressure inside his eight inch shaft. Victoria was getting excited and she began moaning. "I want your cum, Buck. Give me that big load of cum." Buck got more excited and he wanted to release his load. He felt it build up to a massive climax. He did not pull his dick out. He shot all his cum up into Victoria's pussy. When he was finished, he let his dick slide out of her warm pussy. He watched as the load of cum dripped out of her pussy on to the sheet that was covering the sleeper bed. He told Victoria, "I like to watch the cum dribble back out." Victoria slid over on her back and performed a kegel maneuver and a big blob of cum spilled out onto the sheet. It kept coming out. Buck must have given her a big load. It looked like about 3-4 tablespoons of spunk dribbled out of her pussy. It was exciting to Buck to watch it come out. He said I like to feel it going in and watch it coming back out." Victoria was not completely sure what he said, but she could tell he was enjoying watching her. Victoria reached down and rubbed her pussy lips. She got some cum on her finger and put it in her mouth. "UUUmmmmm, tastes good."

Buck said "I hope you take precaution from getting pregnant." Victoria said was not sure she understood what he said. "No comprendez," said Victoia. Buck gave her a quizzical look and made a motion with his hands that would indicate a pregnant stomach. Victoria nodded and said, "No, Buck, I take pill. I be real safe." "Si," said Buck, "bueno."

Buck pulled his shorts back on and said, "Got to keep moving. He climbed back into the driver's seat and hit the road again. They made it as far as Texarkana and Buck was out of driving hours. He pulled into a truck stop and he and Victoria went in and ate the buffet.

Victoria turned a few trucker's heads. She had on a peasant blouse that showed some cleavage and shorts that showed off her good looking legs. She was a very attractive girl which was not too common around a truck stop. Truckers always noticed good looking women and generally had a comment about them. Buck could tell they were jealous of him having such a fine looking woman accompanying him.

After eating, they washed up in the bathroom. When Buck came out, they were two trucker's talking to Victoria. When they saw Buck, they moved away. Buck asked Victoria, "Are they bothering you?" "No," said Victoria, "They show me money to go for them."

"You be careful," said Buck, "I do not want you to go with anybody. You can get hurt." "There is a trucker that has carried hookers off and killed them and left them beside the road."

Buck and Victoria went back to the truck and they made slow passionate love to each other and fell asleep in each others arms. Buck got an early start the next day and they made it to Nashville by the afternoon. Buck stopped at a truck stop on the edge of town and told Victoria he had to drop his trailer at the terminal. He told Victoria that she should not be seen in his truck since it was against the rules to have a rider with you in a Whiteline truck. He told Victoria to stay at the truck stop and wait on him. He would be back in a couple of hours. He gave her some money to get a shower in the truck stop and get something to eat. He told her not to talk to strangers and he would be back for her. Buck left for the terminal which was only a few miles from the truck stop.

Chapter Nine

Charles "Junior" Mitchell had left a trail of bodies all over the country from previous encounters with "lot lizards." He had become quite adept at getting them into his cab, having sex with them, and then choking them and leaving their bodies in a garbage bag all along the interstate highway system. He had lost count of how many there had been. It was somewhere in the neighborhood of 15. He seemed to get more sexually excited with every girl he murdered.

Junior was sitting in his yellow Peterbilt tractor in the truck stop parking lot. He watched Buck and Victoria go into the truck stop. He was mesmerized by Victoria. She was dressed like a truck stop hooker in her tight shorts and peasant blouse. Buck was not sure if she was with Buck or not. He saw them get out of the truck together and he was hoping he could make a play for her. He really thought she was attractive.

Junior followed them into the truck stop and saw Buck say good bye to her. He watched her go into the shower. He sat in the truckers lounge and watched TV until she came back out. She looked tremendous when she came out. She had on a skirt with a fresh clean peasant blouse and when she came close to Junior he could smell her perfumed scent. Junior had to have her.

Victoria went into the restaurant and fixed her a plate from the buffet. She sat down at a vacant table. Junior fixed him a plate and came over to her table and asked if he could join her. Victoria did not say anything so Junior sat down with her.

Junior said, "You are a very pretty girl. Are you with the Whiteline trucker I saw you come in with?"

Victoria understood enough to answer him. She said, "I caught a ride to Nashville. My cousin - I try to telephone." Junior made a bold move when he realized the door might be open for him. "I will give you a lot of money for a date with you on my truck," said Junior as he showed Victoria five – one hundred dollar bills.

Victoria's eyes lit up. This was a lot more money than she was accustomed to getting for the tricks she turned at Nuevo Laredo. She let her desire for the money cloud her better judgement. She did try to see if she could get even more money from this trucker. She held up six fingers and asked, "Six hundred?"

Okay, said Junior, "I will give you six hundred," as he pulled out another hundred dollars in twenties from his billfold.

Victoria could not turn down the cold hard cash. She said, "okay, uno fuck, 30 minutes, no more."

Junior agreed, but he had other plans. They headed for Junior's truck. Victoria had a small bag with some personal belongings. She left them with a security guard and said she would be right back. She got on the truck with Junior and climbed into his sleeper compartment. Junior gave her the money and she began taking her clothes off. Junior said "I need to get a rubber," and he reached down behind the driver's seat in the truck. What Victoria did not know is that he also got a rag full of ether. Junior had tried a lot of different methods to have his way with the girls before he killed them. He preferred to knock the girls out as soon as possible. He got his kicks by having his way with them after they were unconscious. He told Victoria to get on her knees and lean over the bed so he could get behind her and do it "doggie style." She obliged him. She wanted this to be over quickly and she could be on her way with the six hundred dollars. Junior got the rubber on and put his dick in her from behind. He then reached around her and put the ether soaked rag over her mouth until she was out cold. He pounded her hard after she was unconscious and he got more excited than if she were participating. He finished and pulled the rubber off and was careful to put it in his trash bag.

He wanted to get out of the truck stop quickly. He tied her up and gagged her so she would not scream. He pulled out of the parking lot and headed up the interstate. Junior was not through with her. He drove for about an hour out of town and pulled off on a secluded off ramp.

Chapter Ten

Buck drove to the terminal in Nashville and dropped his trailer on the yard. He went to the dispatcher and found out his load was not ready yet. It would not be ready for about 10 hours. Buck took care of some of his personal needs. He took a shower, filled put his log book and turned in his trip logs. He checked his truck out and filled it up with fuel. He thought he would drive back out to the truck stop and see how Victoria was getting along, get a bite to eat and get his truck washed.

When Buck got back to the truck stop, he looked for Victoria and could not find her. He saw her travel bag sitting outside the truck stop next to the wall. He asked a security guard if he had seen Victoria. The security guard said, "Sure, I remember her, a real good looking Mexican girl. She waited right there next to that bag for a while. I saw her talking to a trucker and saw her go in terminal with him. I guess they ate lunch together. They were in there about a half an hour. I saw them come back out and get in the truck together. I thought they were together. They were on the truck for about 15 minutes and then they left together. I thought it was strange that she left her bag behind."

"What kind of truck was it?" Buck asked.

"It was a yellow Peterbilt. He was pulling a flatbed with a roll of steel wire on it. They left about 15 minutes ago. I could not see the girl. She must have been in the sleeper." "What did he look like?" Buck questioned the guard.

"He was a big burly man with a beard."

Buck knew the guy. He was the same one he had run into in Birmingham. "Which way did they go?" Buck asked.

"I watched them leave. They went west on I-40."

"Thank you," Buck said, "If she comes back, tell her to call me. My name is Buck."

Buck ran to his truck. He jumped in and took off. He might be able to catch him since he was bobtail and he was chasing a loaded truck. Buck knew the road and knew he would have to pull a couple of hills going west on I-40. Buck got on his CB hoping the other truck was not in range. Buck keyed his mike and said, "Break 19, Can anyone give me a 20 on a westbound yellow Peterbilt pulling a skateboard with a roll of coil on it?"

He waited for a response, "I think I passed that truck about 10 miles back. Why are you looking for it?"

"I am trying to catch up with it if I can. They left something back at the truck stop and I would like to get it to them."

"He was pulling that hill pretty slow. I think you can catch him if you keep the hammer down, come on back"

"That's a big 10-4. I got the pedal to the metal and plan to keep it there. You did not see any Smokies, did you? Come on."

"I haven't seen a thing since I crossed the Tennessee line, come on"

"10-4, Thank you for the comeback. I will keep rolling, maybe I can catch up with him shortly.

Buck stayed on his CB. "Break 1 9, Anyone got a copy? Come on?" "Yea, go ahead, hand"

"You have got the Rumblestrip. I am west bound at mile marker 224. I am tryng to catch up with a yellow Peterbilt with a skateboard hauling a roll of coil. Have you seen it? Come on."

"Sorry, Rumblestrip, I am ahead of you at mile marker 220 and have not seen your truck. He might be ahead of me. I'll keep an eye out for you. Come on"

Another voice came over the airway, "Rumblestrip, I passed a yellow Peterbilt about 5 minutes ago. He was heading west bound. You should catch him. What do you want with him? Come on."

"He left something back at the truck stop and I want to get it to him if can. Come on back"

Buck was passing everything on the road. He thought he was hot on the trail of the yellow Peterbilt. He wanted to stay on the CB so he would not miss the yellow Peterbilt if it turned off the road. "How about you eastbound? I am heading westbound and looking for a flatbed behind a yellow Peterbilt. Come on"

"How about u Rumblestrip? I saw a flatbed with a coil on it pull on the off ramp at mile marker 215. Is that the truck you are looking for? Come on" "Yea was it a yellow Peterbilt? Come on"

"I think it was. I did not pay a lot of attention to it. Come on"

"Thanks a lot Driver. I am coming up on the off ramp in a few minutes. I'll check it out. Come on"

"Glad I could be of help. Good luck to you."

Buck was contemplating what he would do when he got to the truck. He was not sure what he would do exactly. He knew he wanted to save Victoria though if it was the same guy he had run into in Birmingham, because he knew what he would do to her. Buck had heard about several other truckstop lot lizards winding up missing or worse.

Buck had five more miles until he got to the exit where the driver had seen the truck pull off. Buck kept the hammer down. He pulled off at the exit and looked for the flatbed. He came up the hill at the ramp to the intersection and he saw the flatbed pulled off on the other side of the ramp parked on the side of the ramp. Buck thought it was best if he parked back on the ramp before he crossed over the intersection. He backed up his tractor and parked. He grabbed his head knocker and took off running.

Buck snuck up behind the trailer and he could tell by looking in the rear view mirror that no one was in the driver sear. So the driver must be in the sleeper. Buck climbed up behind the back of the tractor and tried to listen to what was going on inside. The tractor was shaking and he could hear some muffled noises from inside and knew that Victoria was trying to fight off the burly driver. Buck heard the burly driver say "Shut up bitch, you are going to make matters worse if you keep fighting me. Do you hear me? I want to fuck you again." Victoria was trying to scream through a neckerchief that was tied around her head and through her mouth. She could not scream very loud. Buck had to do something. He went around to the passenger side of the tractor and tried the door. It was locked.

Buck took his head knocker and broke the door window glass. He reached into the tractor and grabbed the door handle and opened the door. He heard the burly man say, "What the hell are you doing? Get the fuck out of my truck or you are a dead man." Buck knew he had to move quickly or the driver might be right. Buck saw the driver reaching under the driver seat for a gun he figured. Buck reached over and grabbed his arm. He swung the head knocker at the same time at the driver's head. The driver blocked his swing with one hand and came up with a 9 mm hand gun in his other hand. Buck quickly hit the driver's arm with the billie stick. The driver cried out in pain but he did not drop the gun. He fired a shot that went through the passenger door. Buck dove at the driver and swung the billie stick again at the driver's head. This time it connected and stunned the burly man. Buck then grabbed the hand of the driver and crashed it into the steering wheel and made him drop the gun. The driver reached for the gun and Buck caught him with a right cross to the head and now the driver was seeing stars. Buck hit him again with his knock out punch and it did the trick. The driver was out cold.

Buck looked at Victoria in the back seat and quickly ungagged her and untied her. "Are you all right?"

She was still groggy but she shook her head. "She replied in Spanish that she had been raped and would have surely been killed if he had not come and saved her.

Buck got the idea even though he did not understand what she had said. Buck quickly tied the hands of the driver up tightly with the bindings he had used on Victoria. Buck found the handcuffs the driver had been using on his victims and put them on the driver in addition to the tie downs. He wanted to make sure he would not get loose. He tied his legs up very tightly and then he pulled him out of the truck and stretched him out on the ground.

Victoria was screaming at the man the whole time. She called him every name in the book and then she gave him a few bitch slaps for good measure.

Buck had called 911 and was waiting on the officers. A deputy sheriff showed up quickly and recognized the driver as being a wanted felon for multiple rapes and murders. He told Buck, "There is a warrant out for this man in a yellow Peterbilt in this state and several others. Thank you for apprehending him and holding him for us." He listened to Victoria for a while and then he called in to his headquarters for an interpreter to take down her statement. He never questioned her about her residence status. That might come up later. She might have to return to Mexico after she gave her testimony. Buck hoped that part would work out all right and not get either one of them in trouble. The officer seemed real happy to get their most wanted criminal into custody and he needed Victoria's testimony.

The officer put the driver in the back of his cruiser and by this time there was a highway patrolman and two more deputy sheriffs on the scene. They thanked Buck again and drove away to incarcerate the criminal. Buck found out he went by the name of Charles "Junior" Mitchell. He was wanted in six states for the murder and rape of seven truck stop prostitutes. Buck figured if they knew about seven of them, there was really a lot more probably.

Buck and Victoria went back to the truck stop. When they got there, Victoria's brother was waiting on her. Victoria gave Buck a big hug and went with her brother. She assured Buck that she would not get him in trouble even if she had to go back to Mexico.

Chapter Eleven

Buck had been on the road too long. He was ready to go back to Charlotte for some rest and relaxation. He wanted to go home and see his girlfriend, Lucy. He called Lucy and told her he would be seeing her in a few hours. Lucy said she could not wait to see him. She would have a surprise waiting for him. Buck put the hammer down and headed for Charlotte. He was wondering what the surprise could be.

When Buck got to Lucy's home and she opened the door to let him in, she was only wearing a robe. She gave Buck a big sensual kiss and hugged him tightly. She said, "Come on. Let's go to bed."

"Let me take a quick shower first. I want to be fresh and clean for you."
"Okay, make it quick. I'll be in the bed waiting for you."

"I'll just be a minute."

All Buck had on when he came out of the bathroom was a towel hanging on his fully erect shaft. Buck walked up to the edge of the bed and Lucy pulled the towel off Buck's big dick and placed her mouth on it. She bobbed her head up and down on it for a short while and then she licked it up and down the entire length of it. She had the covers pulled up but she was naked underneath them. Buck climbed in bed and they kissed each other passionately until they were in such a state of arousal, their bodies were aching for each other.

Lucy said, "Go down on me." And Buck gladly obliged. He loved giving oral sex to Lucy. Buck kissed her neck and kept kissing her down the length of her naked body. He kissed her navel and then kissed her all around her love nest but not directly on it or in it. He kissed the inside of her legs and all around her smoothly shaved brazilean pubic mound. He then opened the lips of her beautiful pussy and was quite surprised when he inserted his tongue into the vaginal canal.

Buck said, "Honey, your pussy tastes like chocolate."

"That's your surprise. I put Hershey's chocolate in it for you Sweetheart. How do you like it?"

"I love it. Your pussy always smells and tastes good, but the chocolate makes it extra good. I love you. I really, really love you." And Lucy responded, "I love you too"

Buck went back to work with his tongue in Lucy's pussy. He worked his tongue as far as he could get it in her pussy to try to get all the chocolate out. He really liked the mixture of pussy juice and chocolate. He then pulled her pussy lips apart and licked her clit ever so lightly with his tongue. Buck continued licking her clit and inserted his finger in her warm, wet opening. She began to moan from the pleasure.

Buck wanted to take his time, but he could not wait any longer to put his dick inside her. He got on top of Lucy but held himself up so that his weight was not crushing her. He slowly inserted his dick into her pussy. She was very wet from the oral sex and her natural juices, but she was still so tight, it was difficult to push his big dick into her. Slowly he worked the tip in and moved it back and forth. Gradually he worked about half the length of his shaft into her tight pussy. Buck was being careful not to hurt Lucy by forcing it in too hard.

It must not have been hard enough for Lucy. She was saying, "Harder, fuck me harder. Come on. Don't be afraid. I want it harder and faster." Not wanting to disappoint her, Buck began really thrusting his shaft into her. "That's it. Don't stop. I am going to come." And she did. Within a few minutes, Lucy was shouting, "OOH, OOH, I am coming." Her body was bucking up and down uncontrollably.

Buck knew he was not going to last long very much longer either. It felt too good. He managed to say, "Turn over. I want to fuck you doggie style."

Lucy flipped over and let him fuck her from behind. She liked this position also. Buck stroked her long and slowly. He felt like he we going to explode any second. When he came, it was really intense. He screamed out, "Aah, Aah, it's coming. You are making my dick come. Oh, that's good. That tis sooo good." Buck lay with his dick inside Lucy for several minutes enjoying that peaceful period after a good climax.

Then Lucy broke the silence, "I want you to do something." "What, I'll do anything."

"I want you to lick the come out of my pussy and swallow it. It's just protein." "Okay"

Buck had never done this, but he was eager to try it. He went down on Lucy and licked her opening until he got it all out. Buck swallowed it.

"How did you like it?" Lucy asked.

"I liked licking it out. There was not much taste to it – kinda metallic, maybe. You have swallowed it before. How do you like it?"

Lucy responded, "I never thought it tasted very good. But I convinced myself I was eating protein and it might be good for me. I did not find it to be distasteful."

Buck felt very close to Lucy and realized he really loved her. He was already feeling like he did not want to hit the road again in his big rig, but he knew he had to on Monday morning. It was Friday and he would enjoy being with Lucy for the next couple of days.

Monday morning came and Buck was in his big rig heading west on I-40. He keyed up the mike on his CB and said, "Break 19 for and eastbound. What's it looking like up the road? Come on back"

Immediately a very clear and strong signal came back, "You are clear all the way to the state line. Haven't seen a sign of a bear anywhere. I heard there was a back-up before you get into Knoxville on the west bound side. Maybe it will be clear by the time you get there. Come on."

"Thanks for the come back, *Hand*, This is *Rumblestrip*, I am westbound and down with the hammer down. Have a good day. Come on."

"Same to you, *Rumblestrip*, Keep the pedal to the metal and have a safe trip. Maybe I will catch you on the flip side. I go by *Cool Hand Luke*" over.

Even though Buck hated leaving Lucy this morning, he knew he could not give up his truck driving for at least several more years. He like the adventure of life on the road for the immediate future.

Printed in the United States
by Baker & Taylor Publisher Services